John Ford's 'Tis Pity She's a Whore: A Retelling

David Bruce

Published by David Bruce, 2022.

JOHN FORD'S 'TIS PITY SHE'S A WHORE: A RETELLING

First edition. July 9, 2022.

Copyright © 2022 David Bruce.

ISBN: 979-8201686581

Written by David Bruce.

Table of Contents

Dedication

Dedicated to Carl Eugene Bruce and Josephine Saturday Bruce

My father, Carl Eugene Bruce, died on 24 October 2013. He used to work for Ohio Power, and at one time, his job was to shut off the electricity of people who had not paid their bills. He sometimes would find a home with an impoverished mother and some children. Instead of shutting off their electricity, he would tell the mother that she needed to pay her bill or soon her electricity would be shut off. He would write on a form that no one was home when he stopped by because if no one was home he did not have to shut off their electricity.

The best good deed that anyone ever did for my father occurred after a storm that knocked down many power lines. He and other linemen worked long hours and got wet and cold. Their feet were freezing because water got into their boots and soaked their socks. Fortunately, a kind woman gave my father and the other linemen dry socks to wear.

My mother, Josephine Saturday Bruce, died on 14 June 2003. She used to work at a store that sold clothing. One day, an impoverished mother with a baby clothed in rags walked into the store and started shoplifting in an interesting way: The mother took the rags off her baby and dressed the infant in new clothing. My mother knew that this mother could not afford to buy the clothing, but she helped the mother dress her baby and then she watched as the mother walked out of the store without paying.

***

The doing of good deeds is important. As a free person, you can choose to live your life as a good person or as a bad person. To be a good person, do good deeds. To be a bad person, do bad deeds. If you do good deeds, you will become good. If you do bad deeds, you will become bad. To become the person you want to be, act as if you already are that kind of person. Each of us chooses what kind of person we will become. To become a good person, do the things a good person does. To become a bad person, do the things a bad person does. The opportunity to take action to become the kind of person you want to be is yours.

A Buddhist monk visiting a class wrote this on the chalkboard: "EVERYONE WANTS TO SAVE THE WORLD, BUT NO ONE

WANTS TO HELP MOM DO THE DISHES." The students laughed, but the monk then said, "Statistically, it's highly unlikely that any of you will ever have the opportunity to run into a burning orphanage and rescue an infant. But, in the smallest gesture of kindness — a warm smile, holding the door for the person behind you, shoveling the driveway of the elderly person next door — you have committed an act of immeasurable profundity, because to each of us, our life is our universe."

Educate Yourself
Read Like A Wolf Eats
Be Excellent to Each Other
Books Then, Books Now, Books Forever

***

In this retelling, as in all my retellings, I have tried to make the work of literature accessible to modern readers who may lack some of the knowledge about mythology, religion, and history that the literary work's contemporary audience had.

Do you know a language other than English? If you do, I give you permission to translate this book, copyright your translation, publish or self-publish it, and keep all the royalties for yourself. (Do give me credit, of course, for the original retelling.)

I would like to see my retellings of classic literature used in schools, so I give permission to the country of Finland (and all other countries) to give copies of any or all of my retellings to all students forever. I also give permission to the state of Texas (and all other states) to give copies of this book to all students forever. I also give permission to all teachers to give copies of this book to all students forever.

Teachers need not actually teach my retellings. Teachers are welcome to give students copies of my eBooks as background material. For example, if they are teaching Homer's *Iliad* and *Odyssey*, teachers are welcome to give students copies of my *Virgil's* Aeneid: *A Retelling in Prose* and tell students, "Here's another ancient epic you may want to read in your spare time."

***

According to Charles Lamb, "Ford was of the first order of poets. He sought for sublimity, not by parcels in metaphors or visible images, but directly where she has her full residence in the heart of man; in the actions and sufferings of the greatest minds."

CAST OF CHARACTERS

Male Characters

Friar Bonaventura: Giovanni's mentor.

A Cardinal: Nuncio to the Pope. A Nuncio is a papal ambassador.

Soranzo: a Nobleman. Annabella's suitor and eventual husband. He is 23 years old.

Florio: Citizen of Parma. Father of Annabella and Giovanni.

Donado: Citizen of Parma. Uncle of Bergetto.

Grimaldi: a Roman Gentleman. Annabella's suitor.

Giovanni: Son to Florio.

Bergetto: Nephew to Donado. Annabella's suitor and then Philotis' suitor and fiancé.

Richardetto: Believed to be dead. Disguised as a bearded physician. Hippolita's husband. Also Philotis' uncle.

Vasques: Servant to Soranzo. Vasques is Spanish and has grey hair.

Poggio: Servant to Bergetto.

Bandits.

Female Characters

Annabella: Daughter to Florio. Sister to Giovanni.

Hippolita: Wife to Richardetto. Soranzo's former paramour.

Philotis: Niece to Richardetto. Becomes Bergetto's fiancée.

Putana: Tutoress to Annabella. She is an older woman.

Minor Characters

Officers, Attendants, Servants, Ladies, etc.

The Scene — Parma, Italy.

Notes:

"Giovanni" is pronounced with four syllables.

The name "Putana" is derived from the Italian word for "whore": *puttana*.

"Signior" is a polite title roughly equivalent to "Mr." It is used for persons of rank.

In this society, the word "wench" could be used affectionately. It was not necessarily a negative word.

The word "sirrah" is a term usually used to address a man of lower social rank than the speaker. This was socially acceptable, but sometimes the speaker would use the word as an insult when speaking to a man whom he did not usually call "sirrah." Close friends, whether male or female, could also call each other "sirrah."

CHAPTER 1

— 1.1 —

In Friar Bonaventura's cell, the good friar and Giovanni were in the midst of a serious discussion.

"Dispute and argue no more about this," Friar Bonaventura said, "for know, young man, that these are no school points."

School points are topics proposed for discussion in theological schools.

He continued, "Nice philosophy may tolerate unlikely arguments, but Heaven admits no jest."

"Nice philosophy" is philosophy that makes over-precise distinctions.

"Jest" means both "exception" and "sophistry."

He continued, "Wits, aka educated men, who presumed on wit, aka human intelligence, too much, by striving how to prove with foolish grounds of argumentation and methods of reasoning that there is no God, discovered first the nearest, shortest way to Hell, and they filled the world with devilish atheism.

"Such questions, youth, are foolish. Far better it is to bless the sun than to reason why it shines. Yet He you talk about — God! — is above the sun.

"No more! I may not hear what you say in argument."

"Gentle father," Giovanni said, "to you I have unclasped my burdened soul as if it were a book. I have emptied the storehouse of my thoughts and heart, and I have made myself poor of secrets. I have not left another word untold, which has not spoken all that I ever dared, or think, or know. And yet here is the comfort I shall have?"

The comfort that Friar Bonaventura was saying was available to Giovanni was obedience to God's laws.

Giovanni continued, "Must I not do what all men else may — love?"

Friar Bonaventura said, "Yes, you may love, fair son."

Giovanni said, "Must I not praise that beauty, which, if framed anew, the gods would make a god of, if they had it there, and kneel to it, as I kneel to them?"

Giovanni was worshipping the wrong gods — the pagan gods. These gods are not omnipresent, omniscient, omnibenevolent, or omnipotent.

Shocked, Friar Bonaventura said, "What! Foolish madman!"

Giovanni interrupted, "Shall a peevish, weak sound, a customary form, passed from man to man — a purely manmade convention passed from generation to generation — concerning brother and sister, be a bar between my perpetual happiness and me?

"Say that we had one father, say that one womb — a curse to my joys! — gave both of us life and birth. Are we not, therefore, each to the other bound so much the more by nature? Are we not, therefore, each to the other bound by the links of blood and of reason?"

By "blood," Giovanni meant blood relationship, but in this society the word also meant lust.

He continued, "Indeed, if you will have it, are we not, therefore, each to the other bound even by religion, to be forever one: one soul, one flesh, one love, one heart, one all?"

Friar Bonaventura said, "Stop! Be quiet, you unhappy, unfortunate youth! For you are lost!"

Giovanni said, "Because I am her brother born, shall my joys then be forever banished from her bed?"

Giovanni had fallen in love with his sister, Annabella, and he wanted to have sex with her.

He continued, "No, father. In your eyes I see the change of pity and compassion; from your age, as from a sacred oracle, distills the life of counsel. You are an old man, and you have acquired the essence of judgment. Tell me, holy man, what cure shall give me ease in these extreme circumstances?"

"Repentance, son, and sorrow for this sin," Friar Bonaventura replied. "For you have moved a Majesty above with your unranged — almost — blasphemy."

The word "almost" can modify either "unranged" or "blasphemy," or both. Friar Bonaventura could mean either 1) your unrestrained almost-blasphemy, or 2) your almost-limitless blasphemy, or 3) your almost-limitless almost-blasphemy.

Giovanni said, "Oh, do not speak of that, dear confessor."

"Are you, my son, that miracle of wit," Friar Bonaventura asked, "who once, within these three months, was esteemed throughout Bologna as a wonder of your age?"

Giovanni had been a remarkable scholar at the University of Bologna in Bologna, Italy.

Friar Bonaventura continued, "How the University of Bologna applauded your self-government, behavior, learning, speech, sweetness, and all that could make up a man!

"I was proud of my guardianship, and I chose rather to leave my books than to part with you. I gave up my position at the University of Bologna so I could continue to be with you — but the fruits of all my hopes are lost in you, as you are lost in yourself.

"Oh, Giovanni! Have you left the schools of knowledge so you can converse with lust and death? For death waits on your lust."

The good friar meant spiritual death, but physical death sometimes also occurs in such extreme circumstances.

Friar Bonaventura continued, "Look through the world, and you shall see shine a thousand faces that are more glorious than this idol that you adore. Leave her, and take your choice of these other faces — promiscuity is much less sin than incest, although in such games as those, those who win end up losing."

Giovanni said, "It would be easier to stop the ocean from flowing and ebbing than to dissuade me from pursuing my vows."

A vow can be a solemn promise to God, such as a vow to pursue a holy life. It can also be a promise of fidelity. What Giovanni had vowed was to love his sister; he wanted to have sex with her.

Friar Bonaventura said, "Then I have finished, and in your willful flames I already see your ruin; Heaven is just."

"Will" means desire, including sexual desire.

But he was not finished: He added, "Yet hear my counsel and advice."

Giovanni said, "As I would hear a voice of life."

"A voice of life" is life-saving counsel and advice. It is also a voice that states God's will.

Friar Bonaventura said, "Hurry to your father's house and lock yourself securely and alone within your bedchamber, then fall down on both of your knees and grovel on the ground. Cry to your heart; wash every word you utter in tears, and if it is possible, in tears of blood."

Tears of blood expressed the greatest sorrow.

He continued, "Beg Heaven to cleanse the leprosy of lust that rots your soul. Acknowledge what you are: a wretch, a worm, a nothing. Weep, sigh, pray three times during the day and three times every night. Do this for seven days, and then, if you find no change in your desires, return to me. I'll think about a remedy. Pray for yourself at home, while I pray for you here in my cell.

"Leave now! Take my blessing with you! We have need to pray."

Giovanni said, "All this I'll do to free me from the rod of vengeance, or else I'll swear my fate's my god."

Giovanni's words were ominous. Because of his desire to commit incest, he was willing to worship fate instead of the Christian God.

Christians believe in free will; we have free will and we can use our reason to control our desires. In Canto 5 of the *Inferno*, Dante describes the sinners of Circle 2: These sinners did not control their lust.

On the street in front of Florio's house, Grimaldi and Vasques were arguing. Florio was the father of Giovanni and of Annabella, whom Giovanni had fallen in love with. Grimaldi was a Roman gentleman who wished to marry Annabella, and Vasques was a servant to Soranzo, a nobleman who also wished to marry Annabella. Vasques had drawn his weapon: a rapier.

Vasques said, "Come, sir, stand to your weaponry; prepare to fight. If you prove to be a coward, I'll make you run quickly."

Grimaldi said, "Thou are no equal match for me."

He meant that Vasques was of a lower social status than he was. Grimaldi was a gentleman, while Vasques was a servant. According to the social standards of this culture, Grimaldi could refuse to fight on the grounds that fighting a servant was beneath his dignity.

Grimaldi used "thou" to refer to Vasques. Two good friends could call each other by the informal "thou," or a person of higher social class could call a person of lower social class "thou," as Grimaldi was doing now. Terms such as "thy" and "thee" and "thine" were used in the same way.

Vasques said, "Indeed I never went to the wars to bring home gossip, nor can I play the mountebank for a meal's food and swear I got my wounds on the battlefield."

Of course, Vasques was insulting Grimaldi. A mountebank was a seller of quack medicine; mountebanks frequently told outrageous lies. Vasques was saying that Grimaldi had a reputation as a soldier, but that reputation was based on lies. By telling outrageous lies about his experience as a soldier, Grimaldi was invited to banquets and so got free food.

Vasques continued, "See these grey hairs of mine? They'll not flinch on account of a bloody nose. Will thou attend to this business at hand — this fight?"

Vasques, a servant, had called Grimaldi, a gentleman, "thou."

Insulted, Grimaldi replied, "Why, slave, do thou think I'll balance my reputation with a cast-suit?"

A cast-suit is a servant who wears his master's cast-off clothing.

He added, "Call thy master, he shall know that I dare —"

Vasques interrupted, "— scold like a cot-quean?"

A cot-quean is a cottage-wife, especially one who nags and complains. Applied to a man, the term meant an effeminate man.

Vasques continued, "Being a cot-quean — that's your profession.

"Thou poor shadow of a soldier, I will make thee know my master keeps servants who are thy betters in quality and performance."

"Quality" means birth, or character, or both.

Vasques continued, "Did thou come here to fight or to prattle?"

"Neither, with thee," Grimaldi said. "I am a Roman and a gentleman; I am one who has gotten my honor with the expense of my blood."

He was saying that he had shed blood on the battlefield.

Vasques replied, "You are a lying coward, and a fool. Fight, or by these hilts I'll kill thee."

The hilts were the hilts of his sword, which he had drawn.

He added sarcastically, "My brave lord!"

Then he asked, "You'll fight?"

Grimaldi replied, "Don't provoke me, for if thou do —"

He drew his sword.

Vasques said, "Have at you. Let's fight."

They fought, and Vasques fought much better than Grimaldi.

Florio, Donado, and Soranzo arrived, but separately. Donado was the uncle of Bergetto, who also wanted to marry Annabella. Soranzo was the master, aka boss, of Vasques.

Florio, whose house Grimaldi and Vasques were fighting in front of, asked, "What is the meaning of these violent quarrels so near my doors? Don't you have any other place, except my house, to vent the spleen — the anger — of your disordered bloods? Must I always be haunted with such unrest that will not allow me to eat or sleep in peace at home?

"Is this how you show your love and respect for me, Grimaldi? Bah! You have no love and respect for me!"

Donado said, "And, Vasques, I may tell thee that it is not well to encourage these quarrels; you are always quick to be stirring up contentions."

Annabella and Putana came out on a balcony overlooking the scene. Unnoticed, they listened to the conversation of the others.

Florio asked, "What's the ground of contention? What are you fighting about?"

Soranzo answered, "That, with your patience, signiors, I'll explain. This gentleman, Grimaldi, whom fame and reputation report to be a soldier — for otherwise I would not know that — rivals me in love for Signior Florio's daughter, Annabella. To her ears he always presses his lovesuit, to my disgrace; he thinks that the way to recommend himself to her is to disparage me in his report."

He then said, "But know, Grimaldi, that although, maybe, thou are my equal in thy blood — your birth — yet this behavior of yours reveals a lowness in thy mind; this lowness, if thou were noble, thou would as much disdain, as I do thee for this unworthiness."

He then said, "And on this ground I willed my servant to correct Grimaldi's tongue. I hold a man as base as Grimaldi to be no match for me."

Vasques said, "And if your sudden coming had not prevented us, I would have bled my gentleman Grimaldi's blood under the gills."

This society believed that one treatment that could restore health was bloodletting — that is, bleeding the patient. Grimaldi had gotten angry, and his face was red, showing an excess of choler or anger. To release that excess of anger, Vasques would have cut Grimaldi under his "gills" — that is, he would cut Grimaldi's throat.

He then said to Grimaldi, "I would have wormed you, sir, for running mad."

The "worm" was a small ligament in a dog's throat. People in this society believed that cutting it would prevent rabies.

Grimaldi said, "I'll be revenged, Soranzo."

Vasques said, "You'll be revenged on a dish of warm broth to stay your stomach — do, honest innocence, do! Spoon-meat is a wholesomer diet than a Spanish blade."

"Stay your stomach" means 1) satisfy your hunger or 2) lower your pride.

An "innocent" is a fool.

Spoon-meat is baby food or easy-to-digest food for an invalid.

Grimaldi said, "Remember this! Remember what I said!"

He exited.

Soranzo said after him, "I fear thee not, Grimaldi."

Florio said, "My lord Soranzo, this is strange to me. Why should you storm since you have my agreement to marry my daughter? I have given you my word. You own — possess — her heart, so for what reason would you think that accusations and gossip might mislead her ear?"

He then stated a proverb: "Losers may talk, by law of any game."

In other words, losers are permitted to grumble.

Vasques said, "Yet the villainy of words, Signior Florio, may be such as would make any unspleened dove choleric. Don't blame my lord in this."

Doves are the birds of peace and they are not choleric, aka angry. People in this society can even say that they are unspleened, since this society believed that the spleen is the seat of anger.

Florio said, "Be quieter. Not for all my wealth would I want love for my daughter to cause the spilling of even one drop of blood.

"Vasques, sheathe your sword. Let's end this fight and drink some wine."

Florio, Donado, Soranzo, and Vasques exited.

Putana said to Annabella, "How do you like this, child? Here's threatening, challenging, quarrelling, and fighting on every side, and all is for your sake; you had better look to protecting yourself, you young woman in my charge, or else you'll soon be stolen away as you sleep."

Annabella said, "But, tutoress, such a life gives no happiness to me — my thoughts are fixed on other matters. I wish that you would leave me now!"

"Leave you!" Putana said. "That wish is no marvel. Leave me no leaving, young woman in my charge. Don't even think about me leaving you. This is love outright: You are definitely in love. Indeed, I don't blame you; you have a choice of suitors that is fit for the best lady in Italy."

Annabella requested, "Please do not talk so much."

Putana continued, "Take the worst with the best; there's Grimaldi the soldier, a very well-timbered, aka well-built fellow. They say he's a Roman and a nephew to the Duke Montferrato. They say he did good service in the wars against the Milanese, but indeed, young woman in my charge, I do not like him, even if it is for nothing but his being a soldier. One in twenty of your skirmishing captains will have some privy maim or other that mars their standing upright."

A privy wound is a secret wound and/or a wound to the private parts. "Standing upright" can refer to a penis' erection.

She continued, "I like him all the worse because he crinkles so much in the hams. Although he might serve if there were no more men, yet he's not the man I would choose."

"Crinkles" means 1) bows, or 2) turns aside. Either Grimaldi bows a lot, or during battles he turns aside in fear.

Annabella said, "Bah, how thou prattle!"

Putana continued, "As I am a true, real woman, I like Signior Soranzo well. He is wise, and what is more, he is rich, and what is more than that, he is kind, and what is more than all this, he is a nobleman. Such a man as him, if I myself were the fair Annabella, I would wish and pray for.

"He is also bountiful; besides, he is handsome, and by my truth, I think, he is wholesome; and that's news in a gallant of three-and-twenty. I know that he is liberal with his money."

Readers may be forgiven for thinking that Soranzo had been liberal in giving money to Putana to put in a good word for him to Annabella.

By being wholesome, Soranzo was whole; that is, he had all of his sexual equipment.

Putana continued, "That he is loving, you know; and he is a man surely, else he could never have purchased such a good name and reputation with Hippolita, the lusty widow, in her husband's lifetime."

Soranzo had had an affair with Hippolita while her husband was still alive.

Putana continued, "And if it were only for that report, sweetheart, I wish he were yours!"

To Putana, Soranzo's having an affair with a married woman was something positive, apparently because it showed virility.

She continued, "Commend a man for his qualities and accomplishments, but take a husband as he is a plain, sufficient, naked man, one who is capable of doing what a man ought to do; such a one is for your bed, and such a one is Signior Soranzo, I swear by my life on it."

Annabella said, "Surely this woman took her morning's draught too soon."

In other words, surely Putana began drinking too early this morning; she must be drunk.

Bergetto and Poggio arrived. Bergetto was another suitor who wished to marry Annabella; Poggio was his servant. Donado, who had recently exited, was Bergetto's uncle.

Putana said, "But look, sweetheart, look what thing comes now! Here's another of your ciphers — zeroes, nonentities — to fill up the number of your suitors. Oh, brave old ape in a silken coat! Watch him."

Bergetto was well dressed, but a proverb stated, "An ape is an ape though dressed in scarlet."

Bergetto asked, "Did thou think, Poggio, that I would spoil my new clothes and leave my dinner in order to fight!"

"No, sir," Poggio replied. "I did not take you for so complete a baby."

"I am wiser than that," Bergetto said, "for I hope, Poggio, thou has never heard of an elder brother who was a coxcomb, aka fool. Have thou, Poggio?"

In this society, primogeniture ruled: The eldest brother would inherit the bulk of the father's estate.

Poggio said, "Never indeed, sir, as long as they had either land or money left them to inherit."

A modern proverb states, "Poor people are crazy; rich people are eccentric."

"Is it possible, Poggio?" Bergetto said. "Oh, monstrous!"

He was shocked at the idea of an elder brother with no land or money to inherit.

He continued, "Why, I'll undertake, with a handful of silver, to buy a headful of wit and intelligence at any time, but sirrah, I have another purchase at hand: I shall have the wench, my uncle says. I will just wash my face and change my socks, and then I'll have at her, indeed. I'll charge her."

He then said, "Mark my pace, Poggio! Watch how I move!"

He charged a short distance.

Poggio replied, "Sir."

He then said to himself, "I have seen an ass and a mule trot the Spanish pavane with a better grace, I don't know how often."

The Spanish pavane is a courtly dance.

Bergetto and Poggio exited.

Annabella said, "This idiot haunts me, too."

"Yes, yes, he needs no description," Putana said. "Young woman who is in my charge, the rich magnifico — Signior Donado, Bergetto's uncle — is below with your father, because he means to make this, his cousin, a golden calf. Signior Donado thinks that you will be a right Israelite and fall down before Bergetto immediately, but I hope I have tutored you better."

The Israelites worshipped a golden calf while Moses was absent (Exodus 32).

A golden calf is also a rich fool.

Putana continued, "They say a Fool's bauble is a lady's playfellow."

A Fool's bauble is literally a stick that a Professional Fool, aka jester, carried. Often the top was carved into a head. Metaphorically, a Fool's bauble is the Fool's penis or a dildo.

Putana continued, "Yet you, having wealth enough, need not cast upon the dearth of flesh, at any rate."

Because Annabella had some wealth, she need not marry Bergetto for his wealth. And she need not marry him out of lack of competition for her hand in marriage; other men wanted to marry her.

Putana continued, "Hang him, innocent!"

An innocent is a fool, but here the word applied to Annabella and meant unspoiled and stainless and unspotted.

Giovanni arrived on the street below the balcony where Annabella and Putana stood.

Annabella said, "But look, Putana, look! What blessed shape of some celestial creature now appears! What man is he, who with such sad aspect walks without taking care of himself?"

"Where?" Putana asked.

"Look below," Annabella replied.

"Oh, it is your brother, sweetheart," Putana said.

Annabella said, "What!"

"He is your brother."

Annabella's brother, Giovanni, had been away a long time to study at the University of Bologna, and so she had not recognized him.

"Surely this man is not my brother," Annabella said. "This man is some woeful thing wrapped up in grief; he is some shadow of a man. It's a pity! He beats his breast and wipes his eyes, which are all drowned in tears. I think I hear him sigh. Let's go down to street level, Putana, and learn the cause of his sorrow. I know that my brother, in the love he bears me, will not deny me a share of his sadness. My soul is full of heaviness and fear."

Annabella and Putana exited from the balcony.

"Lost! I am lost!" Giovanni cried to himself. "My Fates who control my life have doomed my death. The more I strive, the more I love; the more I love, the less I hope. I see that my ruin is certain. What judgment or endeavors could apply to my incurable and restless wounds, I thoroughly have examined, but in vain.

"Oh, I wish that it were not according to religion a sin to make our love a god, and worship it! I have even wearied Heaven with prayers. I have dried up the spring of my continual tears. I have even starved my veins with daily fasts. Whatever intelligence or medical knowledge could counsel, I have practiced, but sadly I find all these counsels only dreams and old men's tales told to frighten unsteady youths; I am still the same as I was. Either I must speak, or burst. It is not, I know, my lust that leads me on, but instead it is my fate that leads me on. Let fear and low faint-hearted shame live with slavish people! I'll tell my sister that I love her, even if my heart were valued as the cost of that attempt. Oh! She is coming!"

Annabella and Putana walked over to him.

"Brother!" Annabella said.

Giovanni prayed quietly, "If such a thing as courage dwells in men, you Heavenly powers, now double all that courage in my tongue!"

"Why, brother," Annabella asked, "won't you speak to me?'

"Yes, I will," Giovanni said. "How are you, sister?"

Annabella replied, "However I am, I think you are not well."

"Bless us!" Putana said. "Why are you so sad, sir?"

Giovanni said, "Let me entreat you, leave us for a while, Putana.

"Sister, I want to speak in private with you."

"Withdraw, Putana," Annabella said.

"I will," Putana said.

As she exited, she said to herself, "If this were any other company for her, I should think my absence an office of some credit, but I will leave them together."

In other words, if any man other than Giovanni had wanted to speak in private with Annabella, then Putana would expect a monetary tip. Young men in love would sometimes bribe the chaperones of young women to give them some privacy.

Giovanni said, "Come, sister, let me hold your hand. Let's walk together. I hope you need not blush to walk with me. Here's no one but you and I."

Annabella asked, "What do you mean?"

Giovanni replied, "Indeed, I mean no harm."

"Harm?" Annabella asked.

Giovanni said, "None, in good faith. How are things with thee?"

Annabella thought, *I hope he is not insane.*

Out loud, she replied, "I am very well, brother."

"Trust me, but I am sick," Giovanni said. "I am afraid that being so sick will cost me my life."

"May mercy forbid that!" Annabella said. "That is not so, I hope."

"I think you love me, sister," Giovanni said.

"Yes, you know I do," Annabella replied.

"I know it, indeed," Giovanni said. "You are very beautiful."

Annabella said, "Ah, then I see you have a merry sickness. You mean to make jokes."

Giovanni said, "Whether I have a merry sickness depends on how things turn out.

"The poets lie. I have read that the beauty of Juno's forehead did exceed the beauty of all other goddesses' foreheads, but I dare to swear that the beauty of your forehead exceeds hers, as hers did theirs."

Juno was the wife of Jupiter, king of gods and men — and she was his sister.

Annabella said, "Indeed, this is a pretty game!"

Giovanni replied, "Such a pair of stars as are thine eyes, would, like Promethean fire, if gently glanced, give life to senseless stones."

"Glanced" can meant 1) glimpsed, or 2) struck.

Prometheus stole the means of making fire from the gods. He then used it — striking flint upon metal — to bring to life a human man and a human woman whom he made out of clay.

Annabella said, "You're joking!"

Giovanni said, "The lily and the rose, most sweetly opposed, upon your dimpled cheeks strive for interchange: First your cheeks are white, and then they are red. Such lips as yours would tempt a saint; such hands as yours would make a hermit lascivious."

Annabella asked, "Are you mocking me, or flattering me?"

Giovanni replied, "If you would see a beauty more exact than art can counterfeit, or than nature can frame, look in your mirror, and there behold your own beauty."

"Oh, you are a fine youth!" Annabella said.

Giovanni held out his dagger to her and said, "Here! Take it!"

Annabella asked, "What should I do with it?"

"And here's my breast," Giovanni said. "Strike home! Rip up my bosom, for there thou shall behold a heart in which is written the truth I speak.

"Why do you just stand there?"

"Are you in earnest?" Annabella asked.

"Yes, I am most earnest," Giovanni replied. "You cannot love?"

Annabella asked, "Whom?"

"Me. My tortured soul has felt affliction to the point of death," Giovanni replied. "Oh, Annabella, I am quite undone!"

Undone meant both 1) ruined and 2) unf**ked.

He continued, "The love of thee, my sister, and the view of thy immortal beauty, have untuned all harmony both of my peace and my life. Why don't you strike my dagger in my heart?"

"Forbid it, my just fears!" Annabella said. "If this is true, it would be better that I were dead."

"True!" Giovanni said.

He meant that he was shocked that she could doubt that he loved her, but if Annabella were to commit incest with him, it would be true that it would be better for her — and him — if she were dead.

He continued, "Annabella, it is no time to jest. I have too long suppressed my hidden flames that almost have consumed me. I have spent many a silent night in sighs and groans. I have ran over all my thoughts, despised my fate, reasoned against the reasons of my love, and done all that smooth-cheeked virtue could advise."

"Smooth-cheeked virtue" could mean innocent virtue, as in the case of a youth who is young and innocent and unable yet to grow a beard. Or it could mean clean-shaven and sophisticated or over-sophisticated — think of a bald-faced liar.

He continued, "But I found all useless. It is my destiny that either you must love me, or I must die."

Annabella asked, "Are you saying this seriously?"

"Let some evil soon happen to me," Giovanni said, "if I dissemble anything. If I am misrepresenting my feelings for you, then let evil soon befall me."

"You are my brother, Giovanni," Annabella said.

"You are my sister, Annabella," Giovanni said. "I know this, and I could show you reason why to love so much the more for this. To which intention wise nature first in your creation meant to make you mine; otherwise, to share one beauty in a double soul would have been a foul sin."

According to Neoplatonism, love is the union of two like souls.

He continued, "Nearness in birth and in blood argues only for a nearer nearness in affection."

Christianity would say that because Giovanni and Annabella are so closely related as brother and sister that they ought not have a sexual union, but Giovanni was arguing that their closeness as brother and sister was a reason for them to have the closest relationship. Of course, he was misrepresenting Neoplatonism, which in this definition of love mentioned the union of souls, not of bodies.

Giovanni continued, "I have asked counsel of a representative of the holy church, Friar Bonaventura, who tells me I may love you."

Giovanni was again equivocating. The love that Friar Bonaventura had said was permissible between Giovanni and Annabella was not the kind expressed in a physical union.

He continued, "It is right and just that since I may, I should; and I will — yes, I will. Must I now live, or die?"

Annabella said, "Live; thou have won the battlefield, and without having to fight. What thou have urged me to do, my captive heart had already long ago resolved to do. I blush to tell thee — but I'll tell thee now — for every sigh that thou have spent for me, I have sighed ten for you, and for every tear that you have shed for me, I have shed twenty for you. And I have done these things not so much because I loved, as because I dared not say I loved, nor could I even scarcely dare think it."

"Let not this music of her words be a dream, ye gods," Giovanni said. "For pity's sake, I beg you!"

Annabella knelt and said, "On my knees, brother, even by our mother's dust, I charge you: Do not betray me to your mirth or hate. Love me, or kill me, brother."

Giovanni knelt and said, "On my knees, sister, even by my mother's dust I charge you: Do not betray me to your mirth or hate. Love me, or kill me, sister."

Annabella had referred to "our mother," while Giovanni had referred to "my mother." Annabella had chosen a sharing possessive pronoun, while Giovanni had not.

Annabella asked, "You are telling the truth, then?"

"Truthfully, I tell you that I am telling the truth," Giovanni said, "and so are you, I hope. Say that you believe I'm in earnest."

Annabella said, "I'll swear that you are."

Giovanni said, "And so will I, and by this kiss."

They kissed.

He said, "Once more, and yet once more."

They kissed twice more.

He then said, "Now let's rise."

They stood up.

Giovanni said, "By this exchange of vows, I swear that I would not exchange this minute for Elysium."

An exchange of vows is binding; an exchange of vows can result in a marriage.

Elysium is the pagan Paradise; it is where the good souls go in the Underworld.

He asked, "What must we now do?"

"Whatever you want," Annabella said.

"Come then," Giovanni said. "After so many tears as we have wept, let's learn to court in smiles, to kiss, and to sleep."

He wanted to start a physical, sexual relationship immediately.

— 1.4 —

Florio and Donado stood together on a street and talked. Donado had been trying to convince Florio to have Annabella, Florio's daughter, marry Bergetto, Donado's nephew.

Florio said, "Signior Donado, you have said enough. I understand what you are saying, but I would have you know that I will not force my daughter to marry against her will.

"You see, I have only two children: a son and her. And my son is so devoted to his education that I must tell you truly I fear for his health. Should he miscarry and die before having children, all my hopes for grandchildren rely upon my daughter. As for worldly fortune, I am, I thank my stars, blessed with enough. My care is, how to match her to her liking; she must like the man she marries. I would not have her marry for wealth, but for love, and if she likes your nephew, let him have her. That's all that I can say."

Florio had already agreed to allow Soranzo, whom he believed his daughter loved, to marry Annabella, so it seemed odd that he was now saying that if Annabella liked Bergetto she can marry him, but most likely he knew that Annabella did not like Bergetto and would never marry him.

Donado replied, "Sir, you speak well, like a true father, and, for my part, if the young folks can like each other and agree to marry, I — between you and me — will promise to guarantee my nephew immediately three thousand florins yearly during my life, and after I am dead, I will give him my whole estate. That will provide a financially good life for your daughter."

Florio said, "It is a fair offer, sir; in the meantime, your nephew shall have free passage to commence his lovesuit to my daughter. If he can thrive, he shall have my consent. So for this time I'll leave you, signior."

Florio exited.

Donado said to himself, "Well, there's hope yet, if my nephew would only have wit and intelligence. But he is such a perfect dunce that I am afraid he'll never win the wench."

In this society, the word "wench" could be used affectionately. It was not necessarily a negative word.

He continued, "When I was young, I could have won her love, truly, and so shall my nephew, if he will learn what he ought to do from me.

"I see him coming now at this most opportune time."

Bergetto and Poggio, his assistant, walked toward Donado.

Donado asked, "How are you now, Bergetto, and where are you walking so quickly?"

"Oh, uncle!" Bergetto said. "I have heard the strangest new news that ever came fresh out of the mint — haven't I, Poggio?"

"Yes, indeed, sir," Poggio replied.

Donado asked, "What is the news, Bergetto?"

"Why, look, uncle, my barber told me just now that there is a fellow who has come to town who undertakes to make a mill go without the mortal help of any water or wind, only with sandbags."

In this culture, people were convinced that a perpetual-motion machine could be created.

Bergetto continued, "And this fellow has a strange horse, a most excellent beast, I'll assure you, uncle, my barber says. This horse's head, to the wonder of all Christian people, stands just behind where his tail is. Is it not true, Poggio?"

"So the barber swore, indeed," Poggio said.

Donado asked, "And you are running there to see this horse?"

Bergetto replied, "Yes, indeed, uncle."

Donado asked, "Will you be a fool all your life?"

He knew that the strange horse was a con. At fairs, people who paid to see a horse with its head where its tail ought to be would see a horse with its tail tied to a manger.

Donado continued, "Come, sir, you shall not go. You have more mind to attend a puppet-play than to attend to the business I told you about. Why, thou great baby, will thou never have intelligence? Will thou make thyself a May-game to all the world?"

A May-game is an entertainment; in this context, it is a laughingstock.

Bergetto looked at Poggio, who said, "Answer for yourself, master."

Bergetto answered, "Why, uncle, should I always sit at home, and not go abroad to see what's going on like other gallants? Should I not see fashionable things?"

"To see hobbyhorses!" Donado said.

Some performers in Morris dances wore a costume that made it look as if they were riding a horse. Such "horses" were called hobbyhorses.

He continued, "What wise talk, I ask, had you with Annabella, when you were at Signior Florio's house?"

"Oh, the wench!" Bergetto said. "May God save me, uncle, but I tickled her with a splendid speech so that I made her almost burst her belly with laughing."

There is some unconscious — by Bergetto — sexual innuendo here. The speech can be interpreted as saying that he tickled her between her legs until she became pregnant. Giving birth would be a kind of bursting her belly.

Donado said, "I think you made her laugh, but what speech was it you made to her?"

Bergetto asked, "What did I say, Poggio?"

Poggio said, "Indeed, my master said that he loved her almost as well as he loved Parmesan cheese and he swore — I'll be sworn for him — that she lacked only such a nose as his was, to be as pretty a young woman as any was in Parma."

Donado said, "Oh, gross!"

Bergetto's telling Annabella that he loved Parmesan choose more than he loved her was bad enough, but Donado realized something that Bergetto did not: People who suffered from syphilis sometimes lost their nose, and so Bergetto had unconsciously come close to telling Annabella that she would be the prettiest girl in Parma if she didn't have syphilis.

Bergetto said, "Now, uncle — then she asked me whether my father had more children than myself. And I said no; it would be better that he would have had his brains knocked out first."

"This is intolerable," Donado said.

"Then she asked, 'Will Signior Donado, your uncle, leave you all his wealth?'" Bergetto said.

"Ha!" Donado said. "That was good; did she harp upon that string? Did she stress getting an answer to that question?"

"Did she harp upon that string!" Bergetto said. "Yes, that she did. I answered, 'Leave me all his wealth? Why, woman, he has no other wit; if he had, he would hear about it to his everlasting glory and confusion.'"

If "wit" referred to his father's wit, then if his father had the wit to leave his money to someone other than Bergetto, then Bergetto would say that his father would hear about it to his everlasting confusion, although other people might say that his father would hear about it to his everlasting glory.

If "wit" referred to his father's child, Bergetto himself, then if his father had another wit, aka another child, and the child were intelligent, his father would hear about it to his everlasting glory. But if the child were unintelligent, his father would hear about it to his everlasting confusion.

Bergetto was also unconsciously saying that his father had lacked so much wit, aka intelligence, that he had left Bergetto all his wealth.

Bergetto continued, "'I know,' I said to her, 'that I am his white boy, aka favorite, and I will not be cheated.' And with that, she fell into a great smile, and went away. Yes, I did certainly and fittingly answer her."

"Ah, sirrah," Donado said, "then I see there's no changing of nature. Well, Bergetto, I fear thou will be a complete ass always."

"I should be sorry if that happens, uncle," Bergetto said.

"Come, come home with me," Donado said. "Since you are no better a speaker, I'll have you write to her after some courtly manner, and you shall enclose some rich jewel in the letter."

"Yes, indeed," Bergetto said. "That will be excellent."

"Peace, innocent!" Donado said. "Be silent! This once in my time, I'll set my wits to school. If all should fail, it is only the fortune of a fool."

Donado was intending to write Bergetto's letter to Annabella.

Bergetto said, "Poggio, this will do nicely, Poggio!"

Bergetto was intending to write his own letter to Annabella.

CHAPTER 2

— 2.1 —

Giovanni and Annabella talked together in an apartment in Florio's house. They had just had sex.

"Come, Annabella, no more are you my sister now, but instead you are my love, a name that is more gracious," Giovanni said. "Do not blush, beauty's sweet wonder, but be proud to know that by yielding your virginity to me thou have conquered and inflamed a heart whose tribute is thy brother's life. You have won my heart, and by doing so, you have won my life."

"And my life is now thine," Annabella replied. "Oh, how these stolen pleasures would print a modest crimson blush on my cheeks, had anyone but my heart's delight prevailed over me and won my virginity!"

Giovanni said, "I marvel why the more chaste of your sex should think that the loss of this pretty toy or trifle called maidenhead is so strange, when after it is lost, it is nothing."

One meaning of the word "strange" is "belonging to others rather than to one's own family."

Also, a "strange woman" is a harlot.

One meaning of the word "nothing" is female genitals, aka "no thing."

He added, "And you are still the same."

Annabella said, "It is well for you; now you can talk."

Did she mean that he could boast about his successful seduction?

Giovanni said, "Music as well consists in the ear, as in the playing."

In other words, for music to be music, it is not enough just to play it; someone must hear it.

In part, Giovanni was being bawdy. In this society, "making music" was used as a metaphor for making love. A woman's ear being penetrated by music is like a vagina being penetrated by a penis. The man does the playing when the man is on top of the woman and is actively penetrating her with his penis.

Annabella said, "Oh, you are wanton! Tell about it, you were best to tell about it, so do."

She was joking about his telling others, but she knew that young men often boasted about their sexual conquests.

Giovanni said, "Thou would chide and criticize me if I told."

He then said, "Kiss me."

They kissed.

He said, "Just like this, Jove hung on Leda's neck, and sucked divine ambrosia — the food of the gods — from her lips."

In Greek and Roman mythology, Jupiter, aka Jove, seduced the mortal woman Leda after appearing to her in the form of a swan. A human and a swan having sex with each other is unnatural, as is a brother and a sister having sex with each other.

After having sex with Jupiter, Leda became pregnant.

Giovanni continued, "I do not envy the mightiest man alive; instead, I regard myself, in being the king of thee, as being greater than I would be if I were king of all the world. But I shall lose you, sweetheart."

"But you shall not," Annabella said.

"You must be married, mistress," Giovanni said.

"Mistress" meant both 1) a title of respect for a woman and 2) a woman who has sex with a man she is not married to.

"Yes, to whom?" Annabella asked.

In this culture, women were expected to marry.

Giovanni said, "Someone must have you."

"Have you" meant both 1) marry you and 2) have you sexually.

"You must," Annabella said.

"No, some other man," Giovanni said.

Annabella said, "Now please do not speak like that unless you are jesting, or you'll make me weep in earnest."

Giovanni said, "What? You will not!"

Will not marry? Or will not weep?

He continued, "But tell me, sweet, can thou be so daring as to swear that thou will live for me, and for no other?"

Annabella replied, "By both our loves I dare; for if thou knew, my Giovanni, that and how all suitors seem hateful to my eyes, thou would trust me then."

"Enough," Giovanni said, "I take thee at thy word. Sweet, we must part. Remember what thou have vowed; keep well my heart."

"Will you be gone?" Annabella asked.

"I must," Giovanni said.

"When will you return?"

"Soon."

"See to it that you do," Annabella said.

"Farewell," Giovanni said.

He exited.

"Go where thou will," Annabella said. "In mind I'll keep thee here, and wherever thou are, I know I shall be there."

She called, "Guardian!"

Putana entered the room.

She asked, "Child, how is everything, child? You are well, thank Heaven — is that right?"

Annabella replied, "Oh, guardian, what a paradise of joy have I passed through!"

Putana joked, "No, what a paradise of joy have you passed under!"

Annabella had been under her brother in the missionary position.

Putana said, "Why, now I commend and congratulate thee, my charge. Fear nothing, sweetheart. What does it matter that he is your brother? Your brother's a man, I hope, and I always say that if a young wench feels sexual desire come upon her, let her take anybody — father or brother. All is one. It doesn't matter whom she sleeps with as long as her sexual passion is satisfied."

Annabella said, "I would not have it be known for all the world."

"Nor would I indeed," Putana said, "because of the speech of the people. Except for potentially causing malicious gossip, what you have done is nothing."

Florio called from another room, "Daughter Annabella!"

"Oh, my!" Annabella said. "My father!"

She called, "Here, sir."

She then said to Putana, "Hand me my needlework."

Florio called from another room, "What are you doing?"

Annabella said to Putana, "I am ready; let him come in now."

Putana opened the door.

Florio entered the room, followed by Richardetto, who was wearing the clothing of a doctor of medicine. Carrying a lute, Philotis, his niece, also entered the room.

"So hard at work!" Florio said. "That's well; you waste no time. Look, I have brought you company.

"Here's a man, a learned doctor, lately come from Padua, location of a famous medical school. He is very skilled in medicine; and because I have seen that you have recently been sickly, I entreated this respectable man to visit you sometime. That sometime is now."

Annabella said politely, "You are very welcome, sir."

"I thank you, mistress," Richardetto said. "Loud fame in full and free report has spoken your praise, which is as great for your virtue as for your perfection of beauty and accomplishments. For which I have been bold to bring with me a niece of mine, a maiden, for song and music, one of which perhaps will give you contentment and happiness, if it would please you to know her."

Annabella said, "They are parts — talents — I love, and she is most welcome because of them."

"Thank you, lady," Philotis said.

Florio said to Richardetto, "Sir, now that you know my house, please don't be formal, and if you find that my daughter needs your medical skill, I'll be your paymaster."

"Sir," Richardetto said, "what I am, she shall command."

Florio replied, "You shall bind me to you with ties of gratitude."

He then said to Annabella, "Daughter, I must have some conversation with you about some matters that concern us both."

Florio said to Richardetto, "Good master doctor, please walk inside. We'll desire to have a little of your niece's cunning skill in music. I think my girl has not quite forgotten to touch an instrument; she could have done it. We'll hear them both play music."

Richardetto said, "I'll wait upon you, sir."

— 2.2 —

Soranzo, holding a book, was in a room in his house.

He read out loud:

"*Love's measure is extreme, the comfort pain;*

"*The life unrest, and the reward disdain.*"

Petrarchan love poetry often contained paradoxes.

Soranzo said to himself, "What's this? Look it over again."

He looked at the passage and then said to himself, "It is so; so writes this smooth, licentious poet in his rhymes."

The author of the passage was Jacopo Sannazaro, a love poet.

Soranzo continued talking to himself, "But, Sannazaro, thou lies because if thy bosom felt such oppression as is laid on mine, thou would have kissed the rod that made thee smart. Go to work then, happy muse, and contradict what Sannazaro has in his ill will written."

He wrote:

"*Love's measure is the mean, sweet his annoys [troubles].*

"*His pleasures life, and his reward all joys.*"

The mean in this context is the Golden Mean between Extremes.

He continued, "Had Annabella lived when Sannazaro, in his brief encomium, celebrated Venice, that queen of cities, he had left that verse that gained him such a sum of gold."

Jacopo Sannazaro had written verses in praise of Venice, and he had been monetarily well rewarded for writing them.

Soranzo continued, "And he would have abandoned those verses for only one look from Annabella. He would have written about her, and about her more divine cheeks."

He believed that Annabella's cheeks were more divine than the gold coins that Jacopo Sannazaro had been awarded.

Soranzo continued, "Oh, how my thoughts are —"

Vasques, Soranzo's servant, shouted from another room, "Please stop. By the rules of civility and etiquette, let me give notice that you are coming. I shall be criticized for my neglect of duty and service."

"What rude intrusion interrupts my peace?" Soranzo said loudly. "Can't I have some privacy?"

Vasques said to the intruder or intruders, "Indeed, you are wronging your modesty."

"What's the matter, Vasques?" Soranzo asked. "Who is it?"

Hippolita and Vasques entered Soranzo's room.

Hippolita, who had had an affair with Soranzo, lifted her veil and said, "It is I. Do you know me now?

"Look, perjured man, on her whom thou and thy distracted — maddened and directed toward the wrong person — lust have wronged.

"Thy sensual rage of blood — violent sexual passion — has made my youth a scorn to men and angels, and shall I be now a foil to thy unsated promiscuity?"

A foil is a background against which a jewel stands out more brightly. Hippolita was saying that Soranzo would use his affair with her as a foil against which his other affairs would stand out more brightly.

She continued, "Thou, false wanton man, know that when my reputation for modesty stood free from stain or scandal, all the charms of Hell or sorcery could not prevail against the honor of my more chaste bosom. Thine eyes did plead in tears, thy tongue in oaths, oaths such and so many that a heart of steel would have been wrought to pity, as was mine.

"And shall the conquest of my lawful bed, and shall my husband's death, urged on by his disgrace, and shall my loss of my reputation as a chaste woman all be ill-rewarded with hatred and contempt? No. Know, Soranzo, that I have a spirit that does as much dislike the slavery of fearing thee, as thou do loath the memory of what has passed."

Soranzo began, "But, dear Hippolita —"

"Don't call me 'dear,'" Hippolita said, "nor think with supple words to smooth the grossness of my abuses; it is not your new mistress, your goodly Madam Merchant, who shall triumph on my dejection; tell her thus from me that my birth was nobler and much more honorable."

"Madam Merchant" referred to Annabella, whom Hippolita knew Soranzo was trying to marry. Annabella's family got its money through commerce.

Soranzo said, "You are too violent."

Hippolita said, "You are too double in your dissimulation. See thou this — this clothing, these black mourning garments of suffering? It is thou who are the cause of this; and it is thou who have divorced my husband from his life, and me from him — and you made me a widow in my widowhood."

She believed that she had been widowed twice. Once literally, when her husband had died. And once figuratively, when Soranzo had stopped his affair with her.

Soranzo asked, "Will you listen to me?"

Hippolita said, "Listen to more of thy perjuries? Thy soul is drowned too deeply in those sins — thou need not add to the number."

"Then I'll leave you," Soranzo said. "You are past all rules of sense."

He meant that she was acting against the rules of reason.

Hippolita said, "And thou of grace."

She meant that he had acted and was acting in such a way that put him beyond God's mercy.

Vasques said to Hippolita, "Bah, mistress, you are not close to being within the bounds of reason. Even if my lord had a resolution as noble as virtue itself, you are taking a course of action that unedges, aka blunts, his resolution to do the right thing."

He then said to Soranzo, "Sir, I beg you to not perplex her and drive her to distraction; griefs, unfortunately, will have a vent, an outlet — they will be expressed. I dare to vouch that madam Hippolita will now freely and willingly hear you."

Soranzo said, "Talk to a frantic, raving woman!"

But he asked Hippolita, "Are these the fruits of your love?"

Hippolita replied, "They are the fruits of thy untruth, false man! Didn't thou swear while my husband still lived that thou would wish for no happiness on earth more than to call me your wife? Didn't thou vow that when my husband died that you would marry me? Because of your vows, the devil in my blood and thy protestations caused me to counsel him to undertake a voyage to Ligorne because we had heard that his brother there was dead and he had left behind a daughter who was young and without friends. This daughter, with much effort expended by me to persuade him, I wished him to bring back here. He did as I wished and went; and, as thou know, he died on the journey."

The journey from Parma to Ligorne took the traveler through mountainous, bandit-infested territory.

She continued, "My husband, that unhappy man, bought his death at so high a price, and with my advice! Yet thou, for whom I did it, have forgotten thy vows and have left me to my shame."

Soranzo asked, "Who could help this?"

He meant, *Who could have prevented your husband's death?* But Hippolita deliberately misunderstood him to be saying, *Who could have prevented your unhappiness?*

Hippolita replied, "Who? Perjured man! Thou could, if thou had faith or love."

"You are deceived," Soranzo said. "The vows I made to you, if you remember well, were wicked and unlawful; it would be more sinful to keep them than to break them."

Soranzo and Hippolita had made vows that bound them to get married, but they had made them while Hippolita was still married to a living man. That made them illegal, and as Soranzo said here, immoral.

He continued, "As for me, I cannot mask my penitence and hide that I regret our affair. Think thou how much thou have digressed from honor and modesty in bringing about the death of a gentleman, who was thy husband; he was such a one — so noble in his class, social position, learning, behavior, hospitality, and love — that Parma could not show a more splendid man."

Vasques said to Soranzo, "You do not act well; this was not your promise."

Soranzo had promised to marry Hippolita after her husband died.

"I don't care," Soranzo said. "Let her know her monstrous life. Before I'll be servile to so black a sin, I'll be a corpse."

He said to Hippolita, "Woman, don't come here any more. Learn to repent, and die, for by my honor I hate thee and thy lust. You have been too foul."

He exited.

Vasques said to Hippolita, "This part has been badly acted."

Hippolita said, "How foolishly this beast disregards his fate and shuns the use of that which I now scorn more than I once loved — his love! But let him go. My vengeance shall give me comfort for the woe he has caused me."

She started to leave, but Vasques requested, "Mistress, mistress, madam Hippolita! Please, let me have a word or two with you."

"With me, sir?" she asked.

"Yes, with you, if you please," Vasques replied.

"What is it?"

"I know you are infinitely moved by anger now, and you think you have cause to be angry," Vasques said. "Some cause I confess you have, but surely not as much as you imagine."

"Indeed!"

"Oh you were miserably bitter," he said, "which you followed even to the last syllable; indeed, I swear on my life that you were somewhat too shrewish and outspoken. You could not have met my lord at a worse time since I first knew him; tomorrow, you shall find him a new and different man."

"Well, I shall wait his leisure," Hippolita said.

Vasques said, "Bah, this is not a sincere patience; it comes sourly from you. Truly, let me persuade you for once."

Hippolita thought, *I have a plan, and it shall be enacted, thanks be to this opportunity.*

"Persuade me!" she said out loud. "Persuade me to do what?"

Vasques said, "Visit him in some milder temper. Oh, if you could but master your female anger even a little, how might you win him!"

"He will never love me," Hippolita said. "Vasques, thou have been a too trusty servant to such a master, and I believe thy reward in the end will fall out like mine."

Vasques said, "So perhaps it will, too."

Hippolita said, "Assure thyself it will. Had I one as true, as truly honest, as secret to my counsels, as thou have been to him and his, I should think it a small reward, not only to make him master of all I have, but even of myself."

"Oh, you are a noble gentlewoman!" Vasques said.

He was being ironic.

"Will thou feed always upon hopes?" Hippolita said. "Well, I know thou are wise and see daily what is the reward of an old servant."

"Beggary and neglect," Vasques said.

"True," Hippolita said, "but, Vasques, if thou were mine and would be private to me and my plots, I here protest that I myself and all else that I can call mine would be at thy disposal."

Vasques thought, *I know what you are up to, old mole. I know what you are trying to do. I have the wind of thee.*

When an animal has the wind of something, it smells and detects that thing. A clever hunter can use his or her scent to drive deer into a trap. Or a clever hunter can make sure that the animal does not catch the hunter's scent.

Vasques said out loud, "I am not worthy of it by any desert that could lie within my compass, but if I could —"

"What then?" Hippolita asked.

"I should then hope to live in these my old years with rest and security," Vasques said.

"Give me thy hand," Hippolita said. "Now promise me only thy silence, and thy help to bring to pass a plot I have. And here, in sight of Heaven, I make thee lord of me and my estate once the plot is done."

"Come, you are merry," Vasques said. "You are joking. This is such a happiness that I can neither think nor believe."

"Promise thy secrecy, and it is confirmed," Hippolita said.

Vasques said, "Then here I call our good guardian angels for witnesses that whatsoever your designs are, or against whomsoever, I will not only be a lead actor therein but also never disclose it until after it is done."

Hippolita replied, "I take thy word, and, with that word, I take thee for mine.

"Come then, let's talk more about this now."

She thought, *On this delicious poison my thought shall banquet. Revenge shall sweeten what my griefs have tasted.*

Richardetto and Philotis talked together on a public street.

Richardetto said, "Thou see, my lovely niece, these strange mishaps, how all my fortunes turn to my disgrace, wherein I am but as an onlooker, while others actively contribute to my shame, and I am silent."

"But, uncle," Philotis replied, "how can this disguise you are wearing bring you contentment and happiness?"

Richardetto had disguised himself as a doctor of medicine until he could get his revenge against his wife, Hippolita, who had shamed him by having an affair. As part of his disguise, he wore a beard.

"I'll tell thee, gentle niece," Richardetto replied. "Thy wanton aunt in her lascivious, riotous sexual indulgences now lives overconfident, thinking that she is safe because — she thinks — I am surely dead as a result of my recent journey to Ligorne for you. My 'death' is a rumor that I have caused to be spread.

"Now I want to see with what impudence she gives scope to her loose adultery, and I want to see how the common voice, aka popular opinion, judges her. So far I have prevailed."

Philotis said, "Unfortunately, I fear you mean some strange revenge."

"Oh, don't be troubled by thinking about that," Richardetto said. "Your ignorance shall plead for you in all. Because you don't know what I am planning, you will be innocent of what I am planning. Your ignorance and innocence will protect you.

"But let's turn to our business. This is important! Have you learned for certain that Signior Florio means to give his daughter in marriage to Soranzo?"

"Yes, I learned that for certain," Philotis said.

"But how do you find young Annabella's love inclined toward him?" Richardetto asked. "Does she love him?"

"For all I could tell, she fancies neither him nor anyone else," Philotis replied.

"There's a mystery in that, which time must reveal," Richardetto said. "She treated you kindly?"

"Yes," Philotis replied.

"And she desired your company?"

"Often."

"That is well; it goes as I would wish," Richardetto said. "I am the doctor now, and as for you, no one knows you; if everything does not fail, we shall thrive.

"But who is coming toward us here? I know him; he is Grimaldi, a Roman and a soldier, closely related to the Duke of Montferrato, who is attending on the Nuncio of the Pope. That Nuncio now resides in Parma, and by making use of these connections, Grimaldi hopes to get the love of Annabella."

Grimaldi walked over to Richardetto and said, "May God save you, sir."

"And you, sir," Richardetto said.

Grimaldi said, "I have heard of your proven and approved-of medical skill, which through the city is freely and openly talked about, and I crave your aid."

"Aid for what, sir?" Richardetto asked.

"Indeed, sir, for this matter of mine," Grimaldi replied. "But I want to speak to you in private."

Richardetto said, "Leave us, niece."

Philotis exited.

Grimaldi said, "I love beautiful Annabella, and I want to know whether in the medical arts there may not be recipes for a love potion to persuade her to love me."

"Sir, perhaps there may," Richardetto said. "But these will not at all help you."

"Won't they help me?" Grimaldi asked.

Richardetto said, "Unless I am mistaken, you are a man greatly in favor with the Cardinal."

"What of that?" Grimaldi asked. "How is that relevant?"

Richardetto said, "In duty to his grace, I will be bold enough to tell you that if you seek to marry Florio's daughter, Annabella, you must first remove a barrier between you and her."

"Who is that barrier?"

"Soranzo is the man who has her heart," Richardetto replied, "and while he lives, you can be sure you cannot succeed."

Grimaldi said, "Soranzo! Who, my enemy? Is he the barrier to me achieving my hopes?"

"Is he your enemy?" Richardetto asked.

"He is the man whom I hate worse than damnation," Grimaldi replied. "I will kill him immediately."

"Then take my advice even if it is just for his grace the Cardinal's sake," Richardetto said. "I'll find a time when Soranzo and Annabella will meet, and I'll give you advance notice of that meeting. To be sure that Soranzo shall not escape you, I'll provide a poison for you to dip your rapier's point in; even if Soranzo had as many heads as the Hydra had, he will die."

The Hydra was a mythical monster with many heads. Each time a head was cut off, two more grew in its place.

"But shall I trust thee, doctor?" Grimaldi asked.

"You can trust me as well as you trust yourself," Richardetto replied. "Don't doubt me in anything."

Grimaldi exited.

Alone, Richardetto said to himself, "This shall the Fates decree: Because of me, Soranzo falls — Soranzo who ruined me."

The Fates are three mythological beings who control the length of the lives of human beings. Clotho spins the thread of a human life, Lachesis measures it, and when Atropos cuts the thread, the person dies.

On a public street, Donado, who was carrying a letter, talked with Bergetto and Poggio.

"Well, sir," Donado said, "I must be content to be both your secretary and your messenger. I cannot tell what result this letter may bring, but as sure as I am alive, if thou come once more to talk with her, I fear thou will mar whatsoever good I bring about."

"The good you bring about, uncle!" Bergetto said. "Why, aren't I big enough to carry my own letter, I ask you?"

Donado said, "Yes, yes, you are big enough to carry a fool's head of thy own!"

Jesters, aka professional Fools, carried a scepter at the top of which a head was carved, but the fool's head Donado meant was on Bergetto's shoulders.

Donado continued, "Why, thou dunce, would thou write a letter, and carry it thyself?"

"Yes, that I would," Bergetto replied, "and I would read it to her with my own mouth, for you must think that if she will not believe me myself when she hears me speak, she will not believe another's handwriting. Oh, you think I am a blockhead, uncle. No, sir, Poggio knows I have composed a letter myself, and so I have."

"Yes, truly, sir," Poggio said. "In my pocket I have the letter he wrote."

"It's a sweet letter, no doubt," Donado said. "Please let me see it."

"I cannot read my own handwriting very well, Poggio," Bergetto said. "Read it out loud, Poggio."

Donado said, "Begin."

Poggio read the letter out loud:

"*Most dainty and honey-sweet mistress, I could call you beautiful and lie as quickly as any man who loves you, but because my uncle is the elder man of him and me, I leave it to him, as more fit for his age, and the color of his beard, to lie. I am wise enough to tell you I can both bourd, aka jest, and bourd, aka lay siege to a woman by approaching her, where I see the opportunity. If you like my uncle's wit better than mine, you shall marry me. Or if you like my wit better than his, I will marry you, in spite of the teeth you will bare to me in opposition. So commending my best parts to you, I remain yours,*

"Upwards and downwards, or however you may choose.

"Bergetto."

"Upwards and downwards" is stunningly inappropriate. These are the actions of a penis.

Chances are, Bergetto regarded his penis as one of his "best parts."

Bergetto's use of the word "lie" also inappropriately suggests "lying with," aka "having sex with," Annabella.

Referring to the letter, Bergetto said, "Ah, ha! Here's stuff, uncle!"

By "stuff" he meant content, but Donado probably thought of bullstuff.

"Stuff" can also mean "semen."

can also mean "semen."

Donado said, "Here's stuff indeed — stuff to shame us all. Please tell me whose advice did you take in writing this learnéd letter?"

"None, upon my word," Poggio said, "but my own."

Bergetto's servant, Poggio, was either as foolish as Bergetto, or he enjoyed seeing Bergetto make a fool of himself.

Bergetto said, "And my own advice, uncle, believe it, nobody's else. It was my own brain, I thank a good wit for it."

"Get yourself home, sir," Donado said, "and see to it that you keep inside until I return."

"What!" Bergetto said. "You must be joking! I indeed scorn to return home."

"What!" Donado said. "Don't you scorn my order!"

Bergetto said, "Judge me, but I do scorn it now."

Poggio said, "Indeed, sir, but it is very unhealthy."

If he were speaking to Bergetto, Poggio was saying that crossing his uncle was very unhealthy.

If he were speaking to Donado, Poggio was saying that staying indoors was very unhealthy.

Donado said, "Well, sir, if I hear any of your apish running to puppet shows and follies, until after I come back, you will regret it. You can be sure of that."

He exited.

Bergetto said, "Poggio, shall we steal away and see this horse with the head in its tail?"

"Yes," Poggio said, "but you must beware of being whipped."

"Do you take me for a child, Poggio?" Bergetto asked. "Come, honest Poggio."

In Friar Bonaventura's cell, the good friar and Giovanni were talking.

Friar Bonaventura said, "Peace! Silence! Thou have told a tale whose every word threatens eternal slaughter and damnation to thy soul. I am sorry I have heard it. I wish that my ears had been deaf one minute before the hour that thou came to me!

"Oh, young man cast away and lost and damned, in accordance with the religious members of my order, I day and night have kept awake my aged eyes above and beyond my strength in order to weep on thy behalf.

"But Heaven is angry, and be thou assured, thou are a man who has been marked to endure a misfortune. Look for it; although it may come late, it will come surely."

Giovanni replied, "Father, in saying this you are uncharitable. What I have done, I'll prove to be both fit and good.

"It is a principle that you taught me, when I was still your scholar, that the frame and composition of the mind follows the frame and composition of the body.

"So, where the body's adornment is beauty, the mind's adornment must necessarily be virtue. If this is acknowledged to be true, virtue itself is only refined reason and love is the quintessence — the purest essence — of that.

"This proves that my sister's beauty, being excellently fair, is excellently virtuous: This rare virtue is chiefly in her love — and chiefly, in that love, in her love to me.

"If her love is like that to me, then so is my love to her. This follows because similar causes have similar effects."

Giovanni was making errors in reasoning; he was using the word "love" with the incorrect meaning for this context. The love that is virtuous is different from the love that is sexual passion. *Eros* is sexual love. *Agape* is universal love for all people, including family and strangers, and for God. *Agape* is the love that has the highest virtue. Neoplatonists believed that love is the quintessence — the purest essence — of reason.

He was also associating physical beauty with moral virtue. Unfortunately, some beautiful or handsome people are evil. Nevertheless, Neoplatonists believed in a link between physical beauty and spiritual virtue.

Friar Bonaventura said, "Oh, ignorance in knowledge! Long before this, how often have I warned thee about this before!"

Giovanni was trying to be learnéd, but the errors he was making in argumentation displayed his ignorance.

Friar Bonaventura continued, "Indeed, if we were sure that there were no Deity, that God does not exist, and neither does Heaven nor Hell, then to be led alone by the light of Nature (as were philosophers of the elder times such as Aristotle) might provide some defense.

"But these things are not so: We know that God, Heaven, and Hell exist. So then, madman, thou will find that Nature is blind when it comes to Heaven's tenets."

How do we acquire knowledge? One way is by looking at Nature and trying to understand Nature's laws. Another way is through studying God's revelation as found in the Bible. Friar Bonaventura believed that Giovanni was relying solely on the kind of knowledge that is not revelation. By doing that, he was ignoring knowledge that was directly relevant to determining the kind of relationship — a moral relationship — he ought to have with his sister.

Giovanni said, "Your age overrules you; if you had youth like I do, you'd make her love be your Heaven, and you'd make her divine."

Friar Bonaventura replied, "No, I would not. So now then I see that thou are too far sold to Hell. My prayers for thee are not able to call thee back from Hell, yet let me advise thee. Persuade thy sister to make some marriage."

"Marriage?" Giovanni said. "Why, marriage would damn her! Marriage would prove that she is greedy to experience a variety of lust."

Annabella would then be having sex with both her brother and her husband.

"Oh, fearful!" Friar Bonaventura said. "If thou will not persuade your sister to marry, then give me permission to shrive her and let her confess her sins, lest she should die unabsolved of her sins."

"Shrive her at your best leisure, father," Giovanni replied. "She'll tell you how dearly she prizes my matchless love, and then you will know what a pity it would be that we two should have been sundered from each other's arms.

"View well her face, and in that little round you may observe a world's variety. For color, look at her lips. For sweet perfumes, smell her breath. For jewels, see her eyes. For threads of purest gold, look at her hair. For a delicious choice of flowers, look at her cheeks. Wonder at every portion of that throne that is her face.

"If you just hear her speak, you will swear the spheres are making music for the citizens in Heaven."

This society believed that the planets and the stars are embedded in invisible crystalline spheres that move; as the spheres move, they make the beautiful music of the spheres that we cannot hear in this life.

Giovanni continued, "But, father, those parts of her that are for pleasure framed, lest I offend your ears, shall go unnamed."

Those were the parts between her legs.

"The more I hear, the more I pity thee," Friar Bonaventura said. "That one so excellent should give those parts all to a second death."

The "second death" was damnation. By sleeping with his consent-giving sister, Giovanni was ensuring that her sexual and other parts would be damned.

"Parts" also means qualities. Giovanni had shown intelligence at the university, although his knowledge — as shown by his errors in reasoning — was half-digested. By sleeping with his sister, he was ensuring that his intellectual and other parts would be damned.

"What I can do is only to pray," Friar Bonaventura said, "and yet — I could give you advice, if you would follow it."

Giovanni asked, "What advice?"

"Why, you can still leave her," Friar Bonaventura said. "The throne of mercy is above and beyond your trespass; there is no sin that God cannot forgive if that sin is truly repented. Time is still left for you both —"

Giovanni interrupted, "— to embrace each other. If we cannot embrace each other, then let all time be struck quite out of sequence. Let chaos reign! She is like me, and I am like her; we are resolved and determined to continue our sexual relationship."

"No more of this!" Friar Bonaventura cried. "I'll go and visit her.

"This is what grieves me most: Things being like this means that a pair of souls are lost."

Florio, Donado, Annabella, and Putana talked together in a room in Florio's house.

Florio asked, "Where is Giovanni?"

"He just left," Annabella said. "And I heard him say that he was going to the friar, his reverend tutor."

"Friar Bonaventura is a blessed man," Florio said. "He is a man made up of holiness. I hope the good friar will teach Giovanni how to gain another world."

That world is Heaven.

"Fair gentlewoman," Donado said, "here's a letter sent to you from my young nephew. I dare to swear that he loves you in his soul. I wish that you could hear sometime what I see daily: He sighs and sheds tears as if his breast were a prison to his heart."

"Take the letter, Annabella," Florio said.

"I pity that good man!" Annabella said while taking the letter.

Donado whispered to Putana, "What's that she said?"

Putana whispered, "If it please you, sir, she said, 'I pity that good man!' Truly I recommend him to her every night before her first sleep, because I would have her dream about him; and she listens to my advice most religiously."

The first hours of sleep were those in which young women were thought most likely to experience erotic dreams.

Donado whispered, "Do you say so? God-a-mercy, Putana! Thank you."

"God-a-mercy" means "thank you."

He gave her some money and whispered, "There is something for thee, and please do what thou can on my nephew's behalf; it shall not be lost labor, take my word for it. You will be rewarded for your labor."

"Thank you most heartily, sir," Putana whispered. "Now that I have an understanding of your mind and what you want, I will work to do what you want."

"Guardian," Annabella called.

"Did you call?" Putana replied.

"Keep this letter," Annabella said.

Donado requested, "Signior Florio, in any case have Annabella read the letter immediately."

"Putana keep it!" Florio said to Annabella. "For what? Please read the letter for me here — right now."

"I shall, sir," Annabella replied.

She read the letter silently.

Donado asked Florio, "How do you find your daughter inclined toward my nephew, signior?"

Florio replied, "Truly, sir, I don't know how she is inclined — but it's not at all as well as I could wish."

Annabella said to Donado, "Sir, I am bound to remain your cousin's debtor. The jewel I'll return because if he loves me, I'll count that love as a jewel."

A jewel had been enclosed with the letter, which apparently Donado — not Bergetto — had written.

Donado said, "Do you think that? No, keep them both, sweet maiden. Keep both the jewel and the letter."

"You must excuse me," Annabella said, "but indeed I will not keep the jewel."

Florio asked, "Where's the ring, that ring which your mother, in her will, bequeathed to you, and charged you on her blessing not to give it to anyone but your husband? Send that back to Bergetto."

Annabella replied, "I don't have it."

"Hmm!" Florio said. "You don't have it! Where is it?"

Annabella replied, "My brother this morning took it from me and said that he would wear it today."

"Well, what do you say about young Bergetto's love?" Florio asked. "Are you happy to marry him? Speak."

Donado said, "There is the main point, indeed."

Annabella thought, *What shall I do? I must say something now.*

"What do you say?" her father, Florio, asked. "Why don't you speak?"

Annabella asked, "Sir, with your permission — does it please you to give me freedom to talk frankly, and freedom to choose a husband?"

"Yes, you have that freedom," Florio said.

"Signior Donado, if your nephew intends to raise his fortunes and improve his social position with his marriage, the hope of me — hope of a marriage to me — will hinder such a hope of raising himself," Annabella said. "Sir, if you love him, as I know you do, find a woman more worthy of his choice than me; in short, I'm sure I shall not be his wife."

"Why, here's plain dealing," Donado said. "Here's plain talking! I commend thee for it. And all the worst that I wish for thee is that Heaven bless thee! Despite this, your father and I will still be friends. Shall we not, Signior Florio?"

"Yes, why not?" Florio said. "Look, here your nephew comes."

Bergetto and Poggio walked over to them.

Donado thought, *Oh, the coxcomb! The fool! What is he doing here?*

Bergetto and Poggio were supposed to be at home.

Not seeing Donado's face, Bergetto asked, "Where is my uncle, sirs?"

Donado stepped out from behind one of the others so Bergetto could see him and asked, "What is the news now?"

"May God save you, uncle; may He save you!" Bergetto said. "You must not think I come for nothing, masters; and how, and how is it?"

Seeing Annabella holding a letter, he asked, "Have you read my letter? Ah, there I — tickled you, indeed."

Poggio thought, *But it would be better if you had tickled her in another place.*

He meant between her legs.

Bergetto said to Annabella, "Sirrah sweetheart, I'll tell thee a good jest; and guess what it is."

"You say you'll tell me," Annabella replied.

Bergetto said, "As I was walking just now in the street, I met a swaggering fellow who insisted on walking by the wall where I was walking, and because he thrust me into the street, I very valiantly called him a rogue."

Streets of the time were narrow and had a gutter running down the center. The cleanest place to walk, therefore, was next to the wall by the side of the street. People of a lower class were supposed to move and allow people of a higher class to walk next to the wall. Duels were fought over disagreements about who should walk next to the wall.

Bergetto continued, "He thereupon told me to draw my sword. I told him I had more intelligence than to do that, and when he saw that I would not draw my sword, he did so maul me with the hilts of his rapier that my head sang while my feet capered in the gutter."

Donado thought, *Was there ever such an ass as Bergetto seen!*

"And what did you do all that time?" Annabella asked.

Bergetto said, "I laughed at him for being a fool, until I saw the blood run about my ears, and then I could not choose but find in my heart to cry, until a fellow with a broad beard — they say he is a newly come doctor — called me into his house, and gave me a plaster bandage."

He took off his hat and said, "Look, here it is."

He then said to his uncle, "And, sir, there was a young wench who washed my face and hands most excellently; indeed, I shall love her as long as I live for it."

He then asked, "Didn't she do that, Poggio?"

"Yes, she did, and she kissed him, too," Poggio said.

"Why, now you think I tell a lie, uncle, I bet," Bergetto said.

Donado said, "I wish that he who beat thy blood out of thy head, had beaten some wit and intelligence into it for I fear thou never will have any."

"Oh, uncle, but there was a wench who would have done a man's heart good to have looked on her," Bergetto said. "By this light, she had a face I think worth twenty of yours, Miss Annabella."

Donado thought, *Was there ever a fool born as great a fool as Bergetto?*

"I am glad she liked and pleased you, sir," Annabella said.

"Do you?" Bergetto said. "Truly, I thank you, indeed."

Florio said, "Surely she was the doctor's niece, who was yesterday with us here."

He was referring, correctly, to Richardetto, now disguised as a doctor of medicine, and to Philotis, his niece.

"You are right," Bergetto replied. "It was she. It was she."

"How do you know that, Simplicity?" Donado asked him.

Bergetto said, "Why, didn't Florio say so? If I would have said no, I would have given him the lie, uncle, and so have deserved a dry beating again; I'll have none of that. I don't want to be beaten again."

"To give someone the lie" meant to say that they are lying. In this society, those are fighting words.

A dry beating is a hard beating, especially one that does not draw blood.

Florio said, "She is a very modest well-behaved young maiden, from what I have seen."

"Is she indeed?" Donado asked.

"Indeed she is, if I have any judgment," Florio replied.

Donado said to Bergetto, "Well, sir, now you are free. You need not worry about sending letters now; you are dismissed. The woman — Annabella — you were pursuing here will have none of you."

"She won't!" Bergetto said. "Why should I care about that? I can have wenches enough in Parma for half a crown apiece; can't I, Poggio?"

Poggio said, "Yes, indeed."

Half a crown was twice the going rate for prostitutes, so yes, he could have wenches enough if he paid them that much.

Wanting Bergetto to stop exposing himself as a fool, Donado politely said, "Signior Florio, I thank you for the free access and admittance you gave me in allowing me to speak to Annabella; and to you, fair maiden, that jewel I will give you in anticipation of your marriage to whomever you choose. It's an early wedding present."

He said to his nephew, "Come, will you go, sir?"

Bergetto said, "Yes, indeed I will.

"Miss Annabella, farewell, Miss; I'll come again tomorrow. Farewell, Miss."

Donado, Bergetto, and Poggio exited, leaving behind Florio, Annabella, and Putana.

Giovanni arrived and walked over to them.

Florio asked, "Son, where have you been? Alone, always alone? I wish that you were not always so alone. I would not have it so; you must forsake this over-bookish nature of yours.

"Well, your sister has shook off the fool Bergetto."

Giovanni said, "He was no match for her. Theirs would have been a bad marriage."

Florio said, "They were not well matched, indeed. I never intended for them to be married; Soranzo is the only man I like.

"Look at him, Annabella, and see if he would be a good husband for you.

"Come, it is suppertime, and it grows late."

He exited.

Seeing the jewel Annabella was holding, Giovanni asked, "Whose jewel's that?"

Annabella teased, "Some sweetheart's."

"So I think," Giovanni said.

Annabella teased, "A lusty youth."

Seeing that her brother was upset, she told the truth: "Signior Donado gave it to me to wear as an early wedding present."

"But you shall not wear it," Giovanni said. "Send it back to him again."

Annabella asked, "Are you jealous?"

"That you shall know soon, at better leisure," Giovanni said. "Welcome, sweet night! The evening crowns and completes the day."

CHAPTER 3

— 3.1 —

Bergetto and Poggio spoke together in a room in Donado's house.

"Does my uncle still think to make me a baby?" Bergetto said. "No, Poggio; he shall know I have a head on my shoulders now."

Poggio said, "Yes, let him not put you off like an ape with an apple."

In other words, don't let him bribe you with a trifle to keep you from doing what you want to do, the way that an ape can be bribed with an apple.

Bergetto said, referring to Philotis, "By God's foot, I will have the wench, even if my uncle were ten uncles, in despite of his putting his nose in my business, Poggio."

"Hold him to the grindstone, and give him not a jot of ground," Poggio said. "She has — in a way — promised to marry you already."

"True, Poggio," Bergetto said, "and her uncle, the doctor, swore I should marry her."

"He swore," Poggio said. "I remember."

"And I will have her, what's more," Bergetto said. "Did you see the codpiece-lace she gave me, and the small container of fruit preserves?"

A codpiece is a bag for a man's genitals; a codpiece-lace is a string for tying the codpiece. At this time, codpieces were out of fashion.

Poggio said, "Yes, I saw them very well, and I saw that she kissed you in such a way that my chops watered at the sight of it — I drooled. There is nothing to do except to make a marriage in secret."

"I will do it," Bergetto said, "for I tell thee, Poggio, I begin to grow valiant, I think, and my courage begins to rise."

His courage was not the only thing rising — in this society, "courage" also meant sexual desire.

Poggio asked, "Should you be afraid of your uncle?"

"Hang my uncle, that old doting rascal!" Bergetto said. "No! I say that I will have her!"

"Lose no time then," Poggio said.

Bergetto said, "I will beget a race of wise men and constables who shall cart whores at their own charges."

In this society, constables had the reputation of being slow-witted.

Whores were humiliated by being placed on carts and driven around public areas. Sometimes a whore was whipped as she walked behind the cart. To do this at one's own expense rather than let the public government bear the cost was to show public spiritedness — or a desire for humiliating whores.

Bergetto continued, "And I myself will break the Duke's peace before I have finished.

"Come, let's go."

Florio, Giovanni, Soranzo, Annabella, Putana, and Vasques all talked together in a room in Florio's house.

Florio said, "My lord Soranzo, although I must confess the offers that have been made to me have been great concerning the marriage of my daughter, yet the hope of your still rising honors has prevailed above all other offers.

"Here my daughter is. She knows my mind; speak for yourself to her, and listen, daughter, and see that you treat him nobly.

"I'll give you time to speak together privately.

"Come, son, and all the rest; let us leave them alone so they can agree as they may."

Soranzo said, "I thank you, sir."

Giovanni whispered to Annabella, "Sister, don't be all woman — think about me."

"Don't be all woman" meant "don't be inconstant." A stereotype of women was that they were inconstant in love.

Soranzo said, "Vasques."

"My lord," Vasques answered.

"Wait for me outside."

Everyone exited except Soranzo and Annabella.

Annabella asked, "Sir, what's your will with me? What do you want from me?"

"Don't you know what I am going to say to you?" Soranzo replied.

"Yes," Annabella said. "You'll say you love me."

"And I will swear it, too," Soranzo said. "Will you believe it?"

Annabella replied, "It is not a point of faith."

In other words, it is not something that she has to believe in order to achieve salvation. Also in other words, "It's not something that I have to believe."

Actually, if she were to believe it, marry him, stop sleeping with her brother, and repent her sins, it could help her achieve salvation.

Giovanni appeared on a balcony above them and eavesdropped.

Soranzo asked, "Don't you have the desire to love?"

Annabella replied, "Not to love you."

"Whom then?"

"That's up to the Fates."

Giovanni said to himself, "I'm the regent — the ruler — of the Fates now."

Soranzo asked Annabella, "What do you mean, sweet?"

"I mean to live and die as a maiden," she replied.

"Oh, that's unfit," Soranzo said. "That's not good."

Giovanni said to himself, "Here's one — me — who can say that's only a woman's note. I know that that is not the truth; it's a woman's equivocation."

True, Annabella was equivocating. A maiden is 1) a virgin, and/or 2) an unmarried woman. Annabella was not a virgin, but she was an unmarried woman.

Soranzo said, "If you could only see my heart, then you would swear —"

Taking the words literally, Annabella interrupted, "— that you were dead."

Giovanni said to himself, "That's true, or somewhat near it."

Taken literally, as Annabella had taken Soranzo's words, it is true.

Soranzo asked, "Do you see these true love's tears?"

Annabella replied, "No."

Giovanni said to himself, "Now she has shut her eyes."

"They plead to you for grace and mercy," Soranzo said.

Again taking his words literally, Annabella said, "Yet they say nothing."

Soranzo requested, "Oh, grant my suit."

"What is it?" Annabella asked.

Soranzo said, "To let me live —"

Annabella interrupted, "Take it."

Soranzo finished, "— always yours."

"That is not mine to give," Annabella replied.

Giovanni said to himself, "One more word like that should kill his hopes of marrying her."

Soranzo said, "Miss Annabella, let us put aside these fruitless battles of wit. Know that I have long loved you, and I have loved you truly. Not hope of what you have in material possessions, but hope of having as a wife what you are, has drawn me on. So then let me not in vain still feel the rigor of your chaste disdain. I'm sick, and sick to the heart."

Taking "sick to the heart" literally, Annabella called, "Help, bring some aqua vitae!"

Aqua vitae is brandy or some other medicinal liquor used to revive an ill person.

Soranzo asked, "What do you mean?"

Annabella replied, "Why, I thought that you were sick."

"Do you mock my love?" Soranzo asked.

Giovanni said to himself, "There, sir, she was too nimble and quick-witted."

Soranzo thought, *It is plain; she laughs at me.*

He said to Annabella, "These scornful taunts become neither your modesty nor your youthful years."

"You are no looking glass," Annabella said. "You are no mirror. If you were, I would dress my language by you."

The image was of using a mirror to dress her hair. She meant that she would model her language on his if he were a model to imitate.

In fact, he was not a model to imitate. He had had an affair with a married woman.

Giovanni said to himself, "I am confirmed in my hopes."

Annabella said, "To put you out of doubt and to speak clearly, my lord, I think your common sense should make you understand that if I loved you, or desired your love, to some extent I would have been nicer to you. But since you are a nobleman, and one I would not wish to spend his youth hoping to marry me, let me advise you to stop your courting of me. And please think that I wish you well when I tell you all this."

Soranzo said, "This is what you have to say to me? Is it you who are saying this of your own free will?"

Annabella said, "Yes, I myself am saying this of my own free will. Yet know — to this extent I will give you comfort — if my eyes could have picked out a man, among all those who have courted me, to make a husband of, you would have been that man. Let this suffice. Be noble in your secrecy, and be wise."

Giovanni said to himself, "Why, now I see she loves me."

"One word more," Annabella said. "As ever virtue lived within your mind, as ever noble courses were your guide, as ever you would have me know you loved me, don't tell my father about this ... if I hereafter find that I must marry, it shall be to you or to no one."

"This" was ambiguous. It could mean 1) don't let my father know about how severely I have rejected you, and/or 2) don't let my father know that if I hereafter find that I must marry, it shall be to you or to no one.

This marriage, if it occurred, would be a marriage of convenience; she would still love her brother.

Soranzo said, "I accept that promise."

"Oh," Annabella said. "Oh! My head!"

"What's the matter?" Soranzo asked. "Are you not well?"

"Oh, I begin to sicken," Annabella said.

Giovanni said to himself, "Heaven forbid!"

He exited from the balcony.

"Help, help," Soranzo called. "Those inside there, help!"

Florio, Giovanni, and Putana came running to help.

Soranzo said, "Look after your daughter, Signior Florio."

"Hold her up," Florio said. "She swoons. She is faint."

Giovanni asked, "Sister, how are you?"

"Sick," Annabella said. "Brother, are you there?"

Florio said, "Convey her to bed immediately, while I send for a physician; quickly, I say."

Putana said, "Alas, poor child!"

Everyone exited except Soranzo.

Vasques returned and said, "My lord."

"Oh, Vasques!" Soranzo said. "Now I doubly am undone and ruined, both in my present and my future hopes. She plainly told me that she could not love me, and thereupon she soon sickened, and I fear her life's in danger."

Vasques thought, *By our lady, the Virgin Mary, sir, and so is your life in danger, if you knew all.*

He knew that Hippolita wanted Soranzo dead.

Vasques said out loud, "It's a pity, sir. I am sorry for that. Maybe it is only the maiden's sickness: an overflow of youth."

Young women often suffered from anemia. People in this society believed that the illness stemmed from a readiness for sex, something they lacked until they married.

Vasques continued, "And if that is the case, sir, there is no quicker remedy than a quick marriage. But has she given you an absolute denial?"

"She has, and she has not," Soranzo said. "I'm full of grief. But I'll tell thee what she said as we walk together."

Giovanni and Putana spoke together in another room in Florio's house.

"Oh, sir, we are all ruined, quite ruined, utterly ruined, and shamed forever," Putana said. "Your sister! Oh, your sister!"

"What about her?" Giovanni said. "For Heaven's sake, speak. How is she?"

"Oh, that I was ever born to see this day!" Putana said.

Giovanni asked, "She is not dead, is she?"

"Dead!" Putana said. "No, she is quick."

The word "quick" meant 1) alive, and 2) pregnant.

Putana continued, "It is worse: She is with child. You know what you have done; may Heaven forgive you! It is too late to repent now, Heaven help us!"

She was wrong. According to Christian theology, while one is alive, it is not too late to repent. Also, of course, repentance leads to the help of Heaven.

Giovanni said, "With child? How do thou know that?"

"How do I know that?" Putana said. "Am I at my age ignorant about what qualms and water-pangs mean?"

"Qualms" are feelings of faintness. "Water-pangs" are urges to urinate.

She continued, "Am I ignorant about what the changing of color, queasiness of stomach, puking, and another thing that I could name mean?"

The "another thing" is not menstruating.

She continued, "Do not, for both her and your reputations' sake, spend the time in asking how, and which way — it is so, it is a fact. She is pregnant, upon my word; if you let a physician see her urine and make a diagnosis, you are ruined."

As part of making a diagnosis, physicians examined the patient's urine.

Giovanni asked, "But in what condition is she?"

Putana said, "She is much recovered. It was only a fainting fit, which I quickly saw, and she must expect to experience them often henceforward."

"Commend me to her," Giovanni said. "Tell her not to worry. Don't let the doctor visit her, I order you. Make some excuse until I return.

"Oh, me! I have a world of business in my head. I have many things to do.

"Do not cause her discomfort.

"How this news perplexes me!

"If my father comes to her, tell him she's recovered well. Say it was only food poisoning — do you hear, woman? See that you do it."

— 3.4 —

Florio and Richardetto talked together in another room in Florio's house.

Florio asked, "And how do you find her, sir?"

"Pretty well," Richardetto replied. "I see no danger of death, and I can scarcely perceive she's sick, but she told me that she had recently eaten melons, and she thought that they had disagreed with her young stomach."

"Did you give her any medicine?" Florio asked.

"A mild medicine for indigestion, nothing else," Richardetto replied. "You need not fear for her health; I rather think that her sickness is a fullness of her blood — do you understand me?"

Young female virgins were thought to suffer from an unrequited longing for sex once they were old enough to marry. The remedy was to marry and have sex.

"I do understand," Florio said. "You advise me well. And sometime within these next few days, I will so arrange matters that she shall be married before she knows it."

Richardetto said, "Yet let not haste, sir, result in you making an unworthy choice of a man to be her husband. That would be dishonorable."

"Master doctor, I will avoid doing that," Florio said. "I will not do that. In plain words, my lord Soranzo is the man I mean to marry my daughter."

With conscious irony, Richardetto said, "He is a noble and virtuous gentleman."

With unconscious irony, Florio said, "Yes, as noble and virtuous as any is in Parma.

"Not far from here dwells Father Bonaventura, a grave and serious friar who was once tutor to my son; I'll have Annabella and Soranzo married soon at his cell."

Richardetto said, "You have planned this marriage wisely."

Florio said, "I'll send someone straightaway to speak with him tonight."

"Soranzo's wise," Richardetto said. "He will not delay to marry Annabella."

"That is correct," Florio said. "This marriage will take place quickly."

Friar Bonaventura and Giovanni now walked over to them.

Friar Bonaventura said, "Good peace be here, and love!"

"Welcome, religious friar," Florio replied. "You are one who always brings a blessing to the place you come to."

Giovanni said, "Sir, with what speed I could, I did my best to draw this holy man from forth his cell to visit my sick sister, so that with words of spiritual comfort, in this time of need, he might confess and absolve her, whether she lives or dies."

"This was well done, Giovanni," Florio said. "Thou herein have showed a Christian's care and a brother's love.

"Come, father, I'll conduct you to her chamber, and there is one thing I would entreat you for."

Friar Bonaventura said, "Speak on, sir. What is it you want?"

Florio said, "I have a father's loving notion, and I wish, before I fall into my grave, that I might see Annabella married, as it is fitting and right. A word from you, grave man, will win her more than all our best persuasions. You can persuade her to marry."

Friar Bonaventura replied, "Gentle sir, all this I will say, so that Heaven may prosper her."

Grimaldi stood alone in a room in Richardetto's house.

Grimaldi said to himself, "Now if the doctor keeps his word, Soranzo, twenty to one you will miss marrying your bride. I know it is an ignoble act, and it does not become a soldier's valor, but when it comes to love, where merit cannot sway, a cunning plot must. I am resolved that if this physician is not a double-dealer who is deceiving me, then Soranzo falls."

Richardetto entered the room and said, "You have come at as good a time as I could wish; this very night Soranzo, it is ordained, must be betrothed to Annabella, and, for all I know, married."

"To be betrothed to" means "to be legally engaged to marry someone." A betrothal is a legally binding agreement to marry. A marriage would quickly follow Soranzo and Annabella's betrothal.

Grimaldi said, "What!"

"Yet keep your patience," Richardetto said. "The place the betrothal will happen is in Friar Bonaventura's cell. Now I would wish you to spend this night in watching the cell; it is only a night. But if you miss your opportunity now, tomorrow I'll know all the things I don't know now."

He did not know the time and place of the wedding, although he knew the wedding would happen quickly.

Grimaldi asked, "Do you have the poison?"

"Here it is, in this box," Richardetto said. "Doubt nothing, fear not, this poison will do what it is supposed to do; in any case, as you respect your life, be quick and sure."

Grimaldi said, "I'll speed him on his way to the afterlife."

Richardetto said, "Do so. Leave now, for it is not safe that you should be seen much here. You always have my respect and my love!"

Grimaldi said, "And I give my respect and love to you."

He exited.

Richardetto said to himself, "So! If this succeeds, I'll laugh and metaphorically hug my revenge. And they who now dream of a wedding feast may chance to mourn the lusty bridegroom's ruin.

"But now let me turn to my other business."

He called, "Niece Philotis!"

Philotis entered the room and said, "Here I am, Uncle."

Richardetto asked, "My lovely niece, have you thought about what you will do?"

Philotis replied, "Yes — and as you advised me, I have fashioned my heart to love Bergetto, but he swears he will be married tonight, for he fears that his uncle otherwise, if he should know what is happening, will put a stop to everything, and call Bergetto to shrift and make him repent his actions."

Richardetto said, "Married tonight? Why, that is the best thing that could happen; but let me think … I — ha! — yes … so it shall be. We will put on masks and go in disguise early to the friar's — yes, I have thought about it and that is what we will do."

Philotis said, "Uncle, Bergetto is coming."

Bergetto and Poggio walked over to them.

Richardetto said, "Welcome, my worthy soon-to-be-relative."

"Lass, pretty lass, come kiss me, lass," Bergetto said. "A-ha, Poggio!"

He kissed Philotis.

Philotis thought, *There's hope of this yet. This may yet be a good marriage.*

Richardetto said to Bergetto, "You shall have time enough for kissing. Withdraw with me a little. We must talk at large."

Bergetto asked Philotis, "Have you any sweetmeats or dainty devices for me?"

He was referring to gifts such as those she had previously given to him.

Philotis replied, "You shall have enough, sweetheart."

Such gifts as she meant were given in bed.

Bergetto said, "Sweetheart! Do you hear that, Poggio?"

He then said to Philotis, "By my truth, I cannot choose but kiss thee once more for that word 'sweetheart.'

"Poggio, I have a monstrous swelling about my stomach, whatsoever the matter be."

The swelling was in front, under his belt.

Poggio said, "You shall have medicine for it, sir."

The medicine would be Bergetto's spending his wedding night with Philotis.

"Time runs apace," Richardetto said. "Time is quickly passing."

"Time's a blockhead," Bergetto said.

"Be ruled by me," Richardetto said. "Take my advice. When we have done what's fit to do, then you may kiss her to your fill, and bed her, too."

Annabella and Friar Bonaventura were in her chamber in Florio's house. A table with wax lights was present. As Annabella knelt and confessed her sins to the good friar, who was sitting in a chair, she wept and wrung her hands. Friar Bonaventura's face was serious because he was addressing serious matters.

Friar Bonaventura said, "I am glad to see your penance, for believe me, you have disclosed a soul so foul and guilty that I must tell you truly that I marvel how the earth has borne you up rather than swallowed you to Hell, but weep, weep on. These tears may do you good. Weep faster yet, while I give you a lecture on morality."

Annabella moaned, "Wretched creature!"

Friar Bonaventura replied, "Yes, you are wretched, miserably wretched, almost condemned alive."

In Dante's *Inferno*, some people's souls are being punished in Hell although their bodies, inhabited by demons, still live and move in the Land of the Living. These people were so evil that they were condemned and began to suffer torment in Hell even before they died.

Friar Bonaventura continued, "There is a place — listen, daughter! — in a black and hollow vault, where day is never seen and there shines no sun, but there is a flaming horror of consuming fires, a lightless sulphur, choked with smoky fogs of an infected, poisoned darkness. In this place dwell many thousand thousand sundry sorts of never-dying deaths. There damned souls roar without pity. There gluttons are fed with toads and adders. There burning oil is poured down the drunkard's throat. There the usurer is forced to drink whole draughts of molten gold. There the murderer is forever stabbed, yet he can never die. There the wanton man lies on racks of burning steel, while in his soul he feels the torment of his raging lust."

Annabella cried, "Mercy! Oh, mercy!"

Friar Bonaventura said, "There stand these wretched things, who have dreamed out whole years in lawless sheets and secret incests, cursing one another."

"Lawless sheets" are the sheets on which unlawful lovers such as Annabella and Giovanni lie while committing their secret incest.

Friar Bonaventura continued, "Then you will wish each kiss your brother gave you had been a dagger's point. Then you shall hear how he will cry, 'Oh, I wish that my wicked sister had first been damned when she did yield to lust!' But wait, I think I see repentance work new stirrings in your heart. Tell me, how is it with you? What are you thinking?"

Annabella asked, "Is there no way left to redeem my miseries?"

Friar Bonaventura replied, "Yes, there is, so don't despair — Heaven is merciful and offers grace and mercy to you even now. This is what you must do: First, for your honor's safety, you must marry my lord Soranzo; next, to save your soul, you must leave off this incestuous life of yours and henceforth devote yourself to your husband."

Annabella said, "Ah, me!"

She still passionately loved Giovanni.

Friar Bonaventura said, "Don't sigh. I know the baits of sin are hard to leave; oh, it is like suffering a death to stop enjoying these baits. Remember what must come to you if you continue sinning: eternal damnation. Are you content to marry Soranzo?"

"I am," Annabella said.

Friar Bonaventura said, "I like your answer well; we'll take advantage of the time. This is an opportunity, and we will take advantage of it."

He called, "Who's near us out there?"

Florio and Giovanni entered Annabella's chamber.

"Did you call, father?" Florio asked.

Friar Bonaventura asked, "Has lord Soranzo come?"

Florio replied, "He is waiting below."

Friar Bonaventura asked, "Have you fully acquainted him with everything?"

"I have," Florio said, "and he is overjoyed."

"And so are we," Friar Bonaventura said. "Tell him to come near."

Giovanni asked, "My sister is weeping?"

He thought, *I fear this friar's falsehood.*

To Giovanni, Friar Bonaventura's "falsehood" was advising Annabella to marry.

He said out loud, "I will call Soranzo."

He exited.

Florio asked, "Daughter, are you resolved to marry Soranzo?"

"Father, I am," Annabella replied.

Giovanni returned with Soranzo and Vasques.

Florio said, "My lord Soranzo, here give me your hand; for your hand, I give you this hand."

He joined the hands of Annabella and Soranzo.

Soranzo asked, "Lady, do you agree to marry me, as I agree to marry you?"

Annabella replied, "I do, and I vow to live with you and yours."

This completed the betrothal.

Friar Bonaventura said, "This is timely resolved. Annabella and Soranzo are now legally engaged to be married. My blessing rest on both of them!

"There is more to be done: the wedding ceremony. You two may perform it in the morning's sun."

The wedding would take place during morning daylight hours.

On the street before the monastery in which Friar Bonaventura had a cell, Grimaldi appeared with his rapier drawn and carrying a dark lantern with its shutter closed to conceal its light.

Grimaldi said, "It is early night still, and it is still too soon to finish such a work; here I will lie to listen and find out who comes next."

He lay down with his ear to the ground.

Wearing masks, Bergetto and Philotis arrived. Following them were Richardetto and Poggio.

Bergetto said to Philotis, "We are almost at the place, I hope, sweetheart."

Grimaldi said, "I hear them near, and I heard one say 'sweetheart.' It is Soranzo; now guide my hand, some angry justice, home to his bosom."

He stood up and said, "Now have at you, sir!"

This was an invitation to fight, but he waited for no reply but instead immediately stabbed Bergetto with his poisoned rapier and then fled.

"Oh, help! Help!" Bergetto cried. "Here's a stitch fallen in my guts."

"A stitch fallen" was a phrase used to refer to a tear in clothing. Grimaldi's rapier had ripped a tear in Bergetto's flesh.

"Oh, for a flesh-tailor quickly," Bergetto cried.

A flesh-tailor is a surgeon who can stitch wounds the way that a tailor can stitch clothing.

"Poggio!" Bergetto cried.

Philotis asked, "What ails my love?"

Because of the darkness, she did not know that he had been wounded.

Bergetto said, "I am sure I cannot piss forward and backward, and yet I am wet before and behind."

The wetness on his front and back was blood.

He cried, "Lights! Lights! Ho, lights!"

"Alas, some villain here has slain my love," Philotis said.

Richardetto said, "Oh, Heaven forbid it; raise up the nearest neighbors immediately, Poggio, and bring lights."

Poggio exited to carry out the orders.

"How are you, Bergetto?" Richardetto said. "Slain! It cannot be. Are you sure you are hurt?"

Bergetto replied, "Oh, my belly seethes like a porridge-pot; bring me some cold water, or I shall boil over. My whole body is in such a sweat that you may wring my shirt; feel here — why, Poggio!"

Poggio returned, with officers of the guard, and lights, and said, "Here I am. Alas! How are you doing?"

"Give me a light," Richardetto said. "What's here? All blood! Oh, sirs, Signior Donado's nephew now is slain. Follow the murderer with all possible haste up to the city; he cannot be far from here. Follow the murderer, I beg you."

The officers of the guard cried, "Follow! Follow! Follow!" as they exited.

Richardetto said to Philotis, "Tear off some strips from your linen clothing, niece, so I can use them to stop his wounds."

He then said to Bergetto, "Be of good comfort, man. Be strong."

"Is all this my own blood?" Bergetto said. "Then it is good night with me.

"Poggio, commend me to my uncle, do you hear? Tell him, for my sake, to treat this wench well.

"Oh — I am going the wrong way surely, my belly aches so. I am dying — oh, farewell, Poggio! — oh! — oh!"

He died.

Philotis said, "Oh, he is dead."

"What!" Poggio said. "Dead!"

"He's dead indeed," Richardetto said. "It is now too late to weep: let's take him home, and, with what speed we may, find the murderer."

"Oh, my master!" Poggio grieved. "My master! My master!"

— 3.8 —

Vasques and Hippolita talked together in a room in Hippolita's house.

"Soranzo and Annabella are betrothed?" Hippolita asked. "Betrothed?"

"I saw it done," Vasques replied.

"And when's the marriage day?" Hippolita asked.

"Some two days from now," Vasques replied.

"Two days!" Hippolita said. "Why, man, I wish it were only two hours before I could send him to his last, and lasting, and eternal sleep, and, Vasques, thou shall see I'll do it bravely and splendidly."

"I do not doubt your wisdom," Vasques said, "nor, I trust, do you doubt my secrecy; I am infinitely yours and will keep what you say secret."

Hippolita said, "I will be thine in spite of my disgrace."

The disgrace could be her affair with a married man, Soranzo, while she was married, or it could be the disgrace that would follow from her marrying a servant, Vasques.

"The marriage will take place so soon?" she added. "Oh, wicked man! I dare be sworn that Soranzo would laugh if he saw me weep."

Vasques said, "And that's a villainous fault in him."

"No, let him laugh," Hippolita said. "I am armed in my resolves. Be thou always true."

Vasques said, "I should get little by treachery to you in comparison to what I will get by so hopeful a promotion as I am likely to climb to —"

Hippolita interrupted, "— even to — my bosom, Vasques. Let my youth — Soranzo — revel in these new pleasures of marriage; if we thrive, he now has only a pair of days to live."

Florio, Donado, Richardetto, Poggio, and the officers of the guard stood on the street before the Cardinal's gates.

Florio said, "It is useless now to show yourself to be like a child and weep, Signior Donado. What is done, is done. Don't spend the time in shedding tears, but instead seek for justice."

Richardetto said, "I must confess that I am somewhat in fault because I had not first told you about what love passed between your nephew and my niece, but as I live, his ill fortune and death grieves me as if it were my own."

"Alas, the poor creature," Donado said. "Bergetto meant no man any harm, that I am sure of."

"I believe that, too," Florio said. "But wait, officers of the guard; are you sure you saw the murderer pass here?"

"If it please you, sir," an officer of the guard said, "we are sure we saw a ruffian, carrying a naked weapon all bloody in his hand, get into my lord Cardinal's gate. That we are sure of, but out of fear of his grace — bless us! — we dared go no farther."

Donado asked, "Do you know what manner of man he was?"

"Yes, to be sure, I know the man," the officer of the guard said. "They say he is a soldier. He is a man who loved your daughter, sir, if it please you. It was he for certain."

Florio said, "Grimaldi, on my life."

The officer of the guard said, "Yes, yes, he is the man."

Richardetto said, "The Cardinal is noble; he no doubt will give true justice."

Donado said, "Someone, knock at the gate."

"I'll knock, sir," Poggio said.

He knocked at the gate.

A servant from inside said roughly, "What do you want?"

Florio replied, "We require speech with the lord Cardinal about some urgent business; please inform his grace that we are here."

The Cardinal, followed by Grimaldi, came out of the gate.

"Why, what is this, friends!" the Cardinal said, but his tone made it clear that he did not regard them as friends. "What saucy mates — impudent fellows — are you, who know neither duty nor civility?

"Are we a person fit to be your host, or is our house fit to become your common inn, and so you beat on our doors at your pleasure? What matter of yours requires such haste that it cannot wait for fit times — the daylight hours?

"Are you the magistrates of this community, and yet you know no more discretion than this?

"Oh, your news has arrived here before you; you have lost a nephew, Donado, who this night by Grimaldi was slain. Is that your business?"

His attitude made it clear that he did not regard the death of Donado's nephew as important.

Using the majestic plural, the Cardinal continued, "Well, sir, we have knowledge of it. Let that suffice."

Grimaldi said, "In the presence of your grace, let me say that I never thought or meant to do Bergetto harm.

"But, Florio, you can tell with how much scorn Soranzo, backed with his confederates, has often wronged me. I to be revenged (because I could find no other way to persuade him to fight me) had thought, by way of ambush, to have killed him, but unluckily I mistook Bergetto for Soranzo. If not for that, Soranzo would have suffered what Bergetto so recently felt. And though the fault I did to him was due merely to chance, yet humbly I submit myself to your grace" — he knelt before the Cardinal — "to do with me as you please."

"Rise up, Grimaldi," the Cardinal said.

He rose.

"You citizens of Parma," the Cardinal said, "if you seek for justice, know that as Nuncio — ambassador — from the Pope, for this offence I here receive Grimaldi into his Holiness' protection. He is no common man, but nobly born, of princes' blood, though you, Sir Florio, thought him too mean a husband for your daughter."

The Cardinal was being sarcastic when he called Florio "Sir Florio."

Grimaldi, because he was nobly born, ranked higher socially than Florio and his daughter, although Florio had supported another man — Soranzo, who was also a nobleman — as husband to Annabella.

The Cardinal said, "If you seek more justice for Bergetto's death, you must go to Rome, for Grimaldi shall go thither.

"I advise you to learn more wit and common sense, for shame."

The "shame" lay in trying to get justice for Bergetto's murder. Don't these people realize that the nobly born and the high ranking can do whatever they want!

The Cardinal continued, "Bury your dead.

"Let's go, Grimaldi — let's leave them!"

The Cardinal and Grimaldi exited.

"Is this a churchman's voice?" Donado asked. "Does justice dwell here?"

Florio said, "Justice has fled to Heaven, and comes no nearer to Earth."

Astraea, goddess of innocence, purity, and justice, lived on Earth during the Golden Age, but once the Iron Age arrived, she was sickened by Humankind's new evil and left the Earth to become the constellation Virgo.

Florio continued, "Soranzo! Was this treachery meant for him? Oh, impudence! Had Grimaldi the face to speak it, and not blush?

"Come, come, Donado, there's no help in this, when Cardinals think murder's not amiss. Great men may do their wills, and we must obey, but Heaven will judge them for it, another day."

CHAPTER 4

— 4.1 —

A wedding banquet was set out in a room in Florio's house. Talking together in the room were Friar Bonaventura, Giovanni, Annabella, Philotis, Soranzo, Donado, Florio, Richardetto, Putana, and Vasques.

Friar Bonaventura said, "Now that these holy rites of marriage have been performed, use your time to spend the remnant of the day in feasting. Such fit repasts are pleasing to the saints, who are your guests, though they are not with mortal eyes to be beheld.

"Long prosper as a result of this wedding day to each other's joy, you happy couple!"

Soranzo said, "Father, your prayer has been heard; the hand of goodness has been a shield for me against my death."

Grimaldi had not killed him. The "hand of goodness" is God's providential action, which had protected Soranzo from being murdered by Grimaldi.

Soranzo continued, "And, all the more to bless me, the hand of goodness has enriched my life with this most precious jewel — Annabella is such a prize that Earth has not another jewel like her.

"Cheer up, my love, Annabella, and cheer up, gentlemen, my friends. Rejoice with me in mirth. We'll crown this day with lusty cups of strong wine to Annabella's health."

"This is torture!" Giovanni said to himself. He was jealous that the woman he loved, his sister, was marrying someone else.

He continued, "I wish that the marriage were still undone. Before I'd endure this sight and see my love embraced by another, I would dare destruction and damnation, and I would withstand the horror of ten thousand deaths."

Vasques asked him, "Are you not well, sir?"

"Please, fellow, serve the guests," Giovanni said. "I don't need your special attention."

Florio said, "Signior Donado, come, you must forget your evils that you have suffered and drown your cares in wine."

The recent evils were the murder of Donado's nephew, Bergetto, and the escape from justice by Bergetto's murderer, Grimaldi.

"Vasques!" Soranzo called.

"My lord," Vasques answered.

Soranzo said, "Hand me that weighty goblet."

Vasques got and handed him the goblet.

Soranzo said, "Here, brother–in–law Giovanni, here's to you! Your turn comes next, although now you are a bachelor. Here's to your sister's happiness, and mine!"

He drank, and offered Giovanni the goblet of wine.

"I cannot drink," Giovanni said.

"Why?" Soranzo asked.

"It will indeed offend my stomach," Grimaldi said.

It would also offend him to drink to a marriage he despised.

Annabella said to her husband, Soranzo, "Please do not urge him to drink, if he is not willing."

Oboes sounded.

"What's going on?" Florio asked. "What musical instruments are these?"

Vasques said, "Oh, sir, I forgot to tell you that certain young maidens of Parma, in honor of madam Annabella's marriage, have sent their loves to her in a masque, for which they humbly crave your patience and silence."

A masque is an entertainment in which the performers wear masks.

Soranzo said, "We are much bound to them, so much the more as it is unexpected. Lead in the masked performers."

Hippolita, followed by ladies in white robes with garlands of willows, all masked, entered the room. Because Hippolita, who had had an affair with Soranzo, was masked, she was not recognized.

Willow is a tree that is associated with unrequited love.

Music played, and the masked performers danced.

"Thanks, lovely virgins!" Soranzo said. "Now if we may only know to whom we have been beholden for this kind deed, we shall acknowledge our debt."

"Yes, you shall know," Hippolita said.

She took off her mask and asked, "What do you think now?"

Everyone cried, "Hippolita!"

Normally, people don't want the groom's former mistress to attend the wedding.

Hippolita said, "It is I. Don't be amazed, Soranzo. And don't blush, young lovely bride, I haven't come to defraud you of your man.

"This is now not the time to reckon up the talk that the city of Parma long has rumored about both Soranzo and me. Let rash gossip run on! The breath that vents it will, like a bubble, break itself at last."

She turned to Annabella and said, "But now to you, sweet creature — give me your hand — perhaps it has been said that I would claim some interest in Soranzo, who is now your lord and husband. What right I have to do that, his soul knows best. But in my duty to your noble worth, Sweet Annabella, and my care of you, I say, Soranzo, here, take this hand from me. I'll once more join what the holy church has finished and approved."

Hippolita joined the hands of Soranzo and Annabella.

Hippolita asked Soranzo, "Have I done well?"

Soranzo replied, "You have too much put us in your debt. You are too kind."

"I need to do one thing more," Hippolita said. "So that you may know my pure charity and sincere love, I here freely renounce all interest I ever could claim in Soranzo, and Soranzo, I give you back your vows."

Soranzo had promised to marry her, but now Hippolita was freeing him from that vow.

Earlier, Friar Bonaventura had given Annabella to Soranzo. Now, Hippolita had given Soranzo to Annabella.

Hippolita said, "And to confirm what I say — Vasques, give me a cup of wine."

Vasques gave her a cup of poisoned wine.

She continued, "My lord Soranzo, in this draught I drink I say long rest to you!"

The long rest was death.

She drank and then whispered, "Look to it, Vasques."

This meant for Vasques to poison the wine and give it to Soranzo. Hippolita did not know that Vasques was loyal to Soranzo and had instead poisoned her.

Vasques whispered back, "Fear nothing —"

Soranzo said, "Hippolita, I thank you, and I will pledge this happy agreement as another life."

By "pledge," he meant that he would seal the agreement by drinking wine from the same goblet she had used.

The happy agreement concerned Soranzo's marriage to Annabella. Because he had vowed to marry Hippolita, she could have caused much trouble to that marriage.

He called, "Wine, there!"

Vasques said, "You shall have no wine; neither shall you pledge her."

"What!" Hippolita said.

She had believed that Vasques was going to help her murder Soranzo.

Vasques said, "Know now, mistress she-devil, your own mischievous treachery has killed you; I am not destined to marry you."

"Villain!" Hippolita shouted.

"What's the matter?" people said. "What's the matter?"

Vasques said, "Foolish woman, thou are now like a firebrand that has kindled others and burnt thyself — *troppo sperar, inganna*."

Troppo sperar, inganna is Italian for "too much hoping deceives."

He continued, "Thy vain hope has deceived thee; thou are as good as dead; if thou have any grace, pray."

She had drunk the poisoned wine and would soon be dead; therefore, she had better pray.

Grace is a spiritual gift that enables a person to act virtuously despite original sin.

Hippolita shouted, "Monster!"

Vasques said to her, "Die in charity, for shame. Show some love for other people."

He then said to the other people in the room, "This thing of evil, this woman, has privately attempted to corrupt me with the promise of marriage to her. She has made this cunning and false reconciliation, and she has wanted me to poison my lord, so that she could laugh at his destruction on his marriage day. I promised her that I would do it, but I knew what my reward would have been."

He believed that she would have allowed him to be executed for the murder.

Vasques continued, "I would willingly have spared her life, except that I was acquainted with the danger of her disposition — she was and is too evil to be allowed to live — and now I have given her a just payment in her own coin. There she is, and she has still a short time to live."

He said to her, "Repent, and end thy days in peace, vile woman. As for life, there's no hope that you will live, so don't think it will happen."

All said, "This is wonderful justice!"

Richardetto said, "Heaven, thou are righteous."

Feeling the poison working, Hippolita said, "Oh, it is true that I will die. I feel my time of death coming. Had that slave, Vasques, kept his promise — oh, my torment! — thou, this hour, would have died, Soranzo — heat above Hellfire! — yet, before I pass away — cruel, cruel flames! — take here my curse among you.

"May thy bed of marriage be a rack of torture to thy heart, burn your blood, and boil it in vengeance — oh, my heart, my flame's intolerable — may thou live to father bastards; may her womb bring forth deformed monsters — and die together in your sins, hated, scorned, and unpitied! — oh! — oh!"

She died.

"Was there ever so vile a creature!" Florio said.

"Here's the end of lust and pride," Richardetto said.

"It is a fearful sight," Annabella said.

Soranzo said, "Vasques, I know thee now to be a trusty servant, and I never will forget thee."

He then said, "Come, Annabella, my love. We'll go home, and thank the Heavens for this escape.

"Father and friends, we must break up this mirth. It is too sad a feast."

Donado ordered, "Bear away the body."

Friar Bonaventura said quietly to Giovanni, "Here's an ominous change from celebration to death! Take note of this, my Giovanni, and take heed!

"I fear what may follow. That marriage seldom's good, where the bride-banquet so begins in blood."

Richardetto and Philotis talked together in a room in Richardetto's house.

Richardetto said, "My wretched wife, Hippolita, who was more wretched in her shame than in her wrongs to me, has paid too soon the forfeit of her modesty and life. She died in disgrace.

"And, my niece, I am sure that although vengeance hovers, keeping aloof still from Soranzo's fall, yet he will fall, and sink with his own weight. I need not now — so my heart persuades me — to act to advance his destruction. There is One Above — God — Who begins to work to do that, for I hear that arguments between his wife and him already multiply and rush to a crisis. She, as it is said, denigrates his love, and he abandons her love. Much talk I hear.

"Since things go thus, my niece, in tender love and pity of your youth, my advice to you is that you should free your years from the hazard of these woes by fleeing from here to fair Cremona, where there are many nunneries. There you can vow your soul in holiness and be a holy votaress; you will become a nun.

"Leave me to see the end of these extreme, violent acts. All human worldly courses are uneven, difficult, and unjust. No life is blessed but the life that travels the way to Heaven."

Philotis asked, "Uncle, shall I resolve to be a nun?"

"Yes, gentle niece," Richardetto said, "and in your hourly prayers remember me, your poor unhappy uncle. Hurry to Cremona now, as fortune leads. Your home will be your cloister, your best friends will be your rosary beads, and your chaste and single life shall crown your birth. Who dies a virgin, lives a saint on earth."

Philotis said, "Then farewell, world, and worldly thoughts, adieu! Welcome, chaste vows. I yield myself to you."

In a chamber in Soranzo's house, he and his wife, Annabella, were arguing. In fact, with his jacket unbuttoned, he was dragging Annabella on the floor because he had found out she was pregnant and the baby wasn't his.

He stopped dragging her and said, "Come, strumpet, you famous whore!

"Even if every drop of blood that runs in thy adulterous veins were a life, this sword — do you see it? — would in one blow destroy them all.

"Harlot, rare, notable harlot, who with thy brazen face maintains thy sin, was there no man in Parma to be the pander to your loose cunning whoredom other than I? Must your hot itch and excess of lust, the heyday of your lust, be fed up to an orgasm, and could none but I be picked out to be cloak to your secret tricks — your belly-sports?

"Now I must be the dad to all that gallimaufry — confused jumble that is the sprout of another man's seed — that is stuffed in thy corrupted bastard-bearing womb!

"Why must I?"

Annabella replied, "Beastly man! Why? Because it is thy fate. I did not sue to marry thee; I did not woo thee. But I married you because I thought your over-loving lordship would have run mad and become insane if I had denied you. If you had given me time, I would have told you in what condition I was in — I am pregnant. But you would needs be doing. You wouldn't wait."

"Needs be doing" means "couldn't wait to have sex."

"Whore of whores!" Soranzo said. "Do thou dare tell me this?"

"Oh, yes," Annabella said. "Why not? You were deceived in me; it was not for love I chose you, but to save my reputation. Still, you should know this: Even now if you would be calm and patient, and if you would hide your shame, I'd see whether I could love you."

"Excellent quean!" Soranzo said. "Fine whore! Why, aren't thou with child?"

"What is the need for all this interrogation when it is superfluous?" Annabella said. "I confess that I am pregnant."

"Tell me by whom," Soranzo demanded.

"Stop!" Annabella said. "Telling you that was not included in any agreement I made.

"Still, sir, to appease your appetite for information, I am content to acquaint you with some information. The man, make that the more than man, who begot this sprightly boy — for it is a boy, and therefore you should feel glory, sir, because your heir shall be a son —"

Soranzo interrupted, "Damnable monster!"

This society considered a deformed baby to be a monster, but Soranzo may have been calling Annabella a damnable monster.

Annabella said, "If you will not hear me out, I'll speak no more."

Soranzo replied, "Yes, speak, and speak thy last."

"Agreed! Agreed!" Annabella said. "This noble creature was in every part so angel-like, so glorious, that a woman who is more than human — I myself am only human — would have kneeled before him and have begged him for his love.

"But as for you! Why, you are not worthy once to name his name without true worship, or, indeed, unless you kneeled, to hear another person name him."

Soranzo asked, "What was he called? What is his name?"

"We are not come to that," Annabella said. "Let it suffice that you shall have the glory to father what so brave a father begot."

Soranzo would be the foster father who raises the son of the man who was the boy's biological father.

Annabella continued, "In brief, had not this event fallen out as it has, I never would have been troubled with a thought that you even existed. And as for marriage, I can scarcely even imagine that we are married."

Soranzo ordered, "Tell me his name."

"Alas, alas, there's all I will tell you!" Annabella said. "Will you believe?"

Soranzo asked, "Believe what?"

"That you shall never know," Annabella replied.

"What!" Soranzo said.

"Never shall you know," Annabella said. "If you ever do, then let me be cursed."

"Me not know his name, strumpet!" Soranzo said. "I'll rip up thy heart, and find his name there."

"Do it!" Annabella taunted. "Do it!"

Soranzo added, "And with my teeth, I'll tear the monstrous lecher joint by joint."

"Ha! Ha! Ha!" Annabella said. "The man makes jokes."

"Do thou laugh?" Soranzo said. "Come, whore, tell me the name of your lover, or I swear I'll hew thy flesh to shreds. Who is he?"

Annabella sang, "*Che morte più dolce che morire per amore?*"

The Italian means, "What death is sweeter than to die for love?"

Soranzo said, "Thus I will pull thy hair, and thus I'll drag thy lust-belepered body through the dust."

He dragged her around by her hair and then ordered, "Tell me his name."

Annabella sang, "*Morendo in grazia a lui, morirei senza dolore.*"

The Italian means, "Dying in favor with him, I would die without pain."

Soranzo asked, "Do thou rejoice? The treasure of the earth shall not redeem thee. Even if there were kneeling kings to beg for thy life, or angels came down to plead for you in tears, yet they all would not prevail against my rage. Don't thou tremble now?"

"At what?" Annabella said. "Do I tremble to die! No, be a gallant hangman. I dare thee to do thy worst. Strike, and strike home."

She was insulting him. Being a hangman was a lowly occupation.

She added, "I leave revenge behind, and thou shalt feel it."

She meant that her brother would avenge her death.

Soranzo said, "Yet tell me this before thou dies, and tell me truly: Does thy old father know about this?"

"No, I swear by my life," Annabella said.

"Will thou confess?" Soranzo said. "If you do, I will spare thy life."

"My life!" Annabella said. "I will not buy my life so dear. The price is too high."

Soranzo said, "I will not delay my vengeance."

He drew his sword.

Vasques entered the room and asked, "What do you mean by this, sir?"

"Don't interfere, Vasques," Soranzo said. "Such a damned whore deserves no pity!"

"Now the gods forbid!" Vasques said. "And would you be her executioner, and kill her in your rage, too? Oh, that would be most unmanlike; she is your wife. What faults she has done before she married you were not committed against you."

He continued, "It's a pity! Poor lady, what fault has she committed, which any lady in Italy in the same condition — young and unmarried — would not? Sir, you must be ruled by your reason, and not by your fury; being ruled by your fury would be inhuman and beastly."

"She shall not live!" Soranzo said.

"Come, she must live," Vasques said. "You want her to confess the authors of her present misfortunes, I warrant you."

Only one person had made her pregnant, but Vasques was saying either that Annabella had had many lovers, and/or that she had had assistance in making assignations with her lover or lovers. He may have had in mind Putana.

Vasques continued, "It is an unreasonably excessive demand, and she would lose the estimation that I, for my part, hold of her worth, if she had revealed who had made her pregnant. Why, sir, you ought not, of all men living, to know who made her pregnant. Good sir, be reconciled to her."

He looked at Annabella and said, "Alas, good gentlewoman!"

Annabella said, "Pish, do not beg for me. I value my life as being worth nothing; if the man must be mad and insane, why, then let him take it."

Soranzo asked, "Vasques, do thou hear this?"

Vasques said, "Yes, and I commend her for it. In this she shows the nobleness of a gallant spirit, and curse my heart, but it becomes her rarely."

"Rarely" meant splendidly, but sometimes the word was used ironically.

Vasques whispered to Soranzo, "Sir, in any case and by any means smother your revenge; leave the scenting out of your wrongs to me; take the advice I give you, as you respect your honor, or you will ruin everything."

He was saying that he would discover who had made Annabella pregnant.

He then said out loud, "Sir, if ever my service were of any value to you, then don't be so violent in your disturbance of mind. You are married now, and what a triumph might the report of this give to the other suitors! The suitors of Annabella who were rejected will laugh at you. It is as manlike to bear hardships as it is godlike to forgive."

Soranzo said, "Oh, Vasques, Vasques, in this piece of flesh, this faithless face of hers, I had laid up the treasure of my heart."

Matthew 6:19-21 (King James Version) states this:

19 Lay not up for yourselves treasures upon earth, where moth and rust doth corrupt, and where thieves break through and steal:

20 But lay up for yourselves treasures in Heaven, where neither moth nor rust doth corrupt, and where thieves do not break through nor steal:

21 For where your treasure is, there will your heart be also.

Soranzo said to Annabella, "Had thou been virtuous, you fair, wicked woman, not even the matchless joys of Christian life itself would have made me wish to live with any saint but thee. Deceitful creature, how have thou mocked my hopes, and in the shame of thy lewd womb even buried me alive! I did too dearly love thee."

Vasques said, "This is well."

He whispered to Soranzo, "Follow this tempering of your anger with some passion; be brief and moving. It is for the purpose of getting Annabella to reveal the information you want."

Soranzo said, "Let thy soul and thoughts be witness to my words, and tell me, did thou not think that in my heart I did too superstitiously adore thee?"

By "too superstitiously," he meant idolized — that he treated her like an idol.

"I must confess," Annabella said, "that I know you loved me well."

"And would thou treat me like this!" Soranzo said. "Oh, Annabella, be thou assured that whoever the villain was who thus has tempted thee to this disgrace, he might lust well after thee, but he never loved thee like I love thee. He doted on your beautiful face, which pleased his capricious eye. He did not dote on the part I loved, which was thy heart, and, as I thought, thy virtues."

"Oh, my lord!" Annabella said. "These words wound deeper than your sword could do."

Vasques said, "Let me not ever take comfort, but I begin to weep myself, so much I pity him. Why, madam, I knew, when his rage was over, what it would come to. He again tells you he loves you."

"Forgive me, Annabella," Soranzo said, "although thy youth has tempted thee — above thy strength to resist — to commit folly, yet I will not forget what I should be, and what I am: a husband. In that name 'husband' is hidden divinity."

Ephesians 5:22-24 (King James Version) states this:

22 Wives, submit yourselves unto your own husbands, as unto the Lord.

23 For the husband is the head of the wife, even as Christ is the head of the church: and he is the saviour of the body.

24 Therefore as the church is subject unto Christ, so let the wives be to their own husbands in every thing.

Soranzo continued, "If I do find that thou will yet be true, here I forgive all your former faults, and take thee to my bosom."

Vasques said, "I swear by my truth that that's an example of noble charity."

Annabella knelt and said, "Sir, on my knees —"

"Rise up, you shall not kneel," Soranzo said. "Get you to your chamber, and see that you make no show of alteration. Now that you have repented, see that you don't backslide. I'll be with you straightaway.

"My reason tells me now that it is as common to err in frailty as to be a woman. Go to your chamber."

Annabella exited.

Vasques said, "So! This was somewhat to the purpose. What do you think of your Heaven of happiness now, sir?"

"I carry Hell about with me," Soranzo said. "All my blood is fired with the desire of swift revenge."

Vasques said, "That may be; but do you know how to get revenge, or on whom? Alas! To marry a great woman, being made great in the stock to your hand, is a usual sport in these days."

Annabella was a great lady; she was not working class. She had been made great; she was great in the stock, aka belly, due to being pregnant. And she had been made great to Soranzo's hand, aka beforehand; because she was already pregnant, he did not have to go to the trouble of making her pregnant.

He continued, "But to know what ferret it was that hunted your coney-burrow — there is the cunning."

Many obscene ballads of the time used "ferret" to mean "penis" and "coney" to mean "lady." For example:

"I put it in again.

"It found her out at last.

"The coney then between her legs

"Held my ferret fast."

A burrow is a hole, and so a coney-burrow is a rabbit-hole — or a lady-hole.

"There is the cunning" meant "there is the skill." It would take cunning and skill to find out who had made Annabella pregnant.

Soranzo said, "I'll make her tell herself, or —"

"Or what?" Vasques said. "You must not do so; let me yet persuade you to be patient for a little while. Go to her, and treat her mildly. Win her, if it is possible, to a voluntary confession, to a weeping tune. As for the rest, if all works out OK, I will not miss my mark — I will hit the target.

"Please, sir, go in; the next news I tell you shall be wonders."

Soranzo said, "Delay in vengeance gives a heavier blow."

He exited.

Alone, Vasques said, "Ah, sirrah, here's work for the present occasion! I had a suspicion of a bad matter in my head a pretty while ago, but after my madam's scurvy looks here at home, her waspish perverseness, and loud fault-finding, then I remembered the proverb that where hens crow, and cocks hold their peace, there are sorry houses.

"By God's foot, if the lower parts of a she-tailor's cunning can cover such a swelling in the stomach, I'll never blame a false stitch in a shoe whilst I live again."

A she-tailor is a tailor who makes women's clothing, or perhaps a tailor who is a woman and makes clothing for women. The she-tailor could possibly attempt to cover a pregnancy bump through skillful clothing design.

Vasques said to himself, "Up, and up so quick? And so quickly, too?"

"Up" meant the swelling up of a pregnant woman's belly. "Quick" meant both swift and alive. A live baby was swiftly growing in Annabella's belly.

Vasques said to himself, "It would be a fine piece of cunning to learn by whom Annabella was made pregnant. This must be known; and I have thought about it —"

Putana, in tears, entered the room.

Vasques said to himself, "Here's the way to get the information I want, or none."

He then said out loud to Putana, "What, crying, old mistress! Alas, alas, I cannot blame you; we have a lord, Heaven help us, who is as mad and angry as the devil himself, the more shame for him."

"Oh, Vasques," Putana said, "I regret that I was ever born to see this day! Does he treat thee like this, too, sometimes, Vasques?"

"Me?" Vasques said. "Why, he makes a dog of me, but if some were of my mind, I know what we would do. As sure as I am an honest man, he will go near to kill my lady with unkindness. Say she is with child, is that such a matter for a young woman of her years to be blamed for?"

"Alas, good heart," Putana said. "It is completely against her will. She does not want to be pregnant."

Vasques said, "I dare be sworn that Soranzo's madness is because she will not confess whose baby it is, which Soranzo insists on knowing, and when he knows it, I am so well acquainted with his character and disposition that I know he will forgive and forget everything immediately. I could well wish that she would in plain terms tell all, for that's the way to calm her husband, indeed."

"Do you think so?" Putana asked.

"Oh, I know it," Vasques said, "provided that the father did not win her virginity by force. Soranzo once thought that you could tell him who is the father, and he meant to wring it out of you, but I somewhat pacified him and kept him from doing that, yet I am sure you know a great deal."

"Heaven forgive us all!" Putana said. "I know a little, Vasques."

"Why shouldn't you know?" Vasques said. "Who else should know? I swear upon my conscience Annabella loves you dearly, and you would not betray her to any affliction for the world."

Putana said, "Not for all the world, I swear by my faith and truth, Vasques."

"Your life would be pitiful and contemptible if you would," Vasques said, "but in revealing this information you would relieve her present discomforts, pacify my lord, and gain for yourself everlasting love and preferment."

Putana asked, "Do you think so, Vasques?"

"I know it," Vasques said. "Surely it was some near and entire friend."

"Entire friend" means devoted friend. "Entire" also means with no missing parts; an entire animal is an uncastrated animal.

Putana said, "It was a dear friend indeed, but —"

She hesitated.

"But what?" Vasques said. "Don't be afraid to name him; I will put my own life between you and danger. Indeed, I think it was no base or basely born fellow."

Putana asked, "Thou will stand between me and harm? Will you protect me?"

"By God's pity, what else?" Vasques said. "You shall be rewarded, too, trust me."

Putana said, "The father was even no worse than her own brother."

"Giovanni, her brother, I'll be bound!" Vasques said.

"Even he, Vasques," Putana said. "He is as splendid a gentleman as ever kissed a beautiful lady. Oh, they love most perpetually."

"He is a splendid gentleman indeed!" Vasques said. "Why, in this I commend her choice — better and better."

He whispered to her, "You are sure that he is the father?"

"I am sure," Putana said, "and you shall see that he will not be long away from her, too."

"He would be to blame if he would stay away from her," Vasques said, "but may I believe thee?"

"Believe me!" Putana said. "Why, do thou think that I am a Turk or a Jew? Am I a lying infidel? No, Vasques, I have known their dealings for too long to lie about them now."

"Where are you?" Vasques shouted. "There, within, sirs!"

Some bandits entered the room.

Putana asked, "What is this? Who are these men?"

"You shall know soon," Vasques said. "Come, sirs, take this old damnable hag, gag her instantly, and put out her eyes, quickly, quickly!"

"Vasques!" Putana screamed. "Vasques!"

"Gag her, I say," Vasques said. "By God's foot, do you allow her to babble? Why are you fumbling around? Let me come to her."

"I'll help your old gums, you toad-bellied bitch!"

He gagged her.

Vasques then said, "Sirs, carry her secretly into the coal-house, and put out her eyes immediately. If she roars, slit her nose. Do you hear me? Be speedy and sure."

The bandits exited with Putana.

Alone, Vasques said, "Why this is excellent, and above expectation — her own brother! Oh, horrible! To what a great freedom to commit damnable sins has the devil trained, educated, and enticed our age! Her brother! Well!

"This is still only a beginning. I must go to my lord and tutor him better in his points of vengeance. Now I see how a smooth tale goes beyond and outwits a smooth tail."

He meant that a plausible story outwits a wanton woman. A "smooth tail" is a lubricated vagina.

Vasques then said, "Wait! Listen! What thing comes next? Giovanni! Just as I could wish! My belief is strengthened; it is as firm as winter and summer. Giovanni is the father just as surely as one season succeeds another."

Giovanni walked over to Vasques and asked, "Where's my sister?"

Vasques said, "She is troubled with a new sickness, my lord; she's somewhat ill."

"She took too much of the flesh, I believe," Giovanni said.

He meant that she had eaten too much, but "to take too much of the flesh" had an additional meaning of "to have too much sex." "Flesh" can mean penis.

Vasques said, "Truly, sir, and I think you have definitely hit the mark."

"Hit the mark" meant both 1) "are correct" and 2) "have entered the vagina."

He continued, "But my virtuous lady —"

"Where is she?" Giovanni asked.

Vasques said, "In her chamber, if it would please you to visit her; she is alone."

Giovanni gave him some money. It was a tip for letting him know where she was, but readers may be forgiven if they thought of a whoremonger giving money to a pander for access to a prostitute.

Vasques said, "Your liberality has doubly made me your servant, and ever shall, always."

"Liberality" has two meanings: 1) generosity, and 2) lechery.

Giovanni exited.

Soranzo walked over to Vasques.

"Sir, I am a made man," Vasques said. "I have done what I said I would do. I have plied my cue with cunning and success."

He had been like an actor who gave another actor a cue that caused the other actor to speak. By saying the right things to Putana, he had caused her to reveal to him the information that Soranzo wanted.

Vasques said to Soranzo, "I beg you to let us talk in a private area where we know that we won't be overheard."

"My lady's brother's come," Soranzo said. "Now he'll know all."

Annabella would tell him how Soranzo had treated her.

"Let him know it," Vasques said. "I have made some of them secure enough."

Putana was not now a threat, and since Vasques knew that Giovanni was the father, he could use that information against him.

He asked, "How have you dealt with my lady?"

"Gently, as thou have advised me," Soranzo said. "Oh, my soul runs circular in sorrow for revenge."

He wanted revenge, but he felt like he wasn't getting anywhere. He was like an animal tied at the stake.

Soranzo added, "But, Vasques, thou shalt know."

Vasques interrupted, "Nay, I will know no more, for now comes your turn to know — I have information to give to you. I would not talk so publicly with you. Let my young master, Giovanni, take time enough, and go at pleasure."

He thought that Giovanni and Annabella were having sex in her bedchamber.

"Giovanni's soul has been sold to death, and the devil shall not allow him to be ransomed," Vasques said. "Sir, I beseech you, look out for your privacy. Let us talk together somewhere private."

Soranzo said, "No conquest can gain glory of my fear. Whatever victory my enemy wins, my enemy will not win glory from my fear because I will show none."

CHAPTER 5

— 5.1 —

Annabella appeared at a window above the street in front of Soranzo's house.

Alone, Annabella said to herself, "Pleasures, farewell, and farewell to all the spiritually unprofitable minutes wherein false joys have spun a weary life! Now I take my leave of these my fortunes. Thou, precious Time, that swiftly rides at full speed over the world, to finish up the race of my last fate, here stop thy restless course, and bear to ages that are yet unborn a wretched, woeful woman's tragedy! My conscience now stands up and testifies against my lust, with depositions charactered in guilt."

"Depositions" are written testimony. Letters written in gilt are designed to draw attention to themselves.

Friar Bonaventura arrived and stood below Annabella's window and listened to her.

Annabella continued, "My conscience also tells me I am lost. Now I confess. Beauty that clothes the outside of the face is cursed if it is not clothed with grace.

"Here like a turtledove, confined in a cage, unmated, I converse with air and walls and sing and complain about my vile unhappiness."

Turtledoves are known for being faithful to their mate.

She continued, "Oh, Giovanni, you who have had the spoil and despoliation of your own virtues and of my reputation for modesty, I wish that thou had been less subject to those luckless stars that reigned at my nativity! Oh, I wish that the scourge that is due to my black offence might pass from thee, so that I alone might feel the torment of an uncontrolled fire!"

The "uncontrolled fire" is 1) the fire of passion, and 2) Hellfire.

Friar Bonaventura said to himself, "What's this I hear?"

Annabella said, "That man, that blessed friar, who joined in ceremonial knot — marriage — my hand to Soranzo, whose wife I now am, told me often that I trod the path to death, and he showed me how. But they who sleep in lethargies and moral laxness of lust hug their destruction, making Heaven 'unjust.' And so did I."

God will forgive all sins if they are sincerely repented. But those who embrace their sins do not repent and so are sentenced to Hell eternally. Eternal damnation can seem unjust to such sinners.

Friar Bonaventura, hearing Annabella's repentance, said to himself, "Here's music to the soul!"

Annabella said, "Forgive me, my good guardian angel, and for this once be helpful to my purposes; let some good man pass this way, to whose trust I may commit this paper, double lined with tears and blood. I wrote the words in blood, and my tears splashed on the page. This being granted, here I solemnly vow repentance and a leaving of that lustful life I long have died in."

Annabella meant that she had spiritually died while committing sin.

In this culture, "to die" also meant "to have an orgasm" as well as the usual meaning.

Friar Bonaventura said out loud, "Lady, Heaven has heard you and has by providence ordained that I should be God's minister for your benefit."

Not recognizing his voice, Annabella asked, "Who are you?"

Friar Bonaventura replied, "Your brother's friend, the friar. I am glad in my soul that I have lived to hear this free confession between your peace and you. What do you want me to do with the paper? Do you want me to deliver it to someone? Don't be afraid to speak."

"Is Heaven so bountiful?" Annabella said. "Then I have found more favor than I hoped. Here, holy man."

She threw down the paper, which was a letter.

She then said, "Commend me to my brother. Give him that — that letter. Tell him to read it, and repent. Tell him that I, imprisoned in my chamber, barred from all company, even from my guardian, Putana — which gives me reason to suspect much — have time to blush at what has passed. Tell him to be wise and not believe the friendship of my lord and husband, Soranzo. I fear much more than I can speak. Good father, the place is dangerous, and spies are busy. I must stop speaking. Will you do it? Will you deliver the letter and my words to my brother?"

"Be sure that I will, and be sure that I will fly with speed," Friar Bonaventura replied. "May my blessing always rest with thee, my daughter; live, in order to die more blest!"

He exited.

Alone, Annabella said to herself, "Thanks to the Heavens, who have prolonged my breath and allowed me to live for this good purpose! I have repented, and I have advised my brother to repent. Now I can welcome death."

— 5.2 —

Soranzo and Vasques talked together in another room in Soranzo's house.

"Am I to be believed now?" Vasques said. "First, marry a strumpet who casts herself away upon you only to laugh at your horns!"

Invisible horns were said to grow upon the forehead of cuckolds — husbands who had unfaithful wives.

He continued, "She wants to feast on your disgrace, take delight in your vexations, cuckold you in your bride-bed, waste your estate upon panders and bawds —"

Soranzo interrupted, "No more, I say! No more!"

"A cuckold is a comely tame beast, my lord!" Vasques said.

"I am resolved," Soranzo said. "I have made up my mind. Don't say another word. My thoughts are pregnant and will give birth to revenge, and my thoughts are all as resolute as thunder.

"In the meantime, I'll cause our lady and wife to dress herself in all her bridal robes — her wedding dress. I will kiss her, and clasp her gently in my arms.

"Leave now — but first answer this: Are the bandits ready to lie in wait for an ambush?"

"Good sir," Vasques said, "don't worry about any other business than your own resolution to get revenge; remember that time once lost cannot be recalled."

"With all the cunning and persuasive words thou can," Soranzo said, "invite the statesmen of Parma to my birthday feast. Hasten to my brother-in-law rival and his father — Giovanni and Florio. Entreat them gently to come to the feast, and tell them not to fail to appear. Be speedy, and then return."

"Don't let your pity betray you," Vasques said. "Until I come back, think upon incest and cuckoldry."

Soranzo said, "Revenge is all the ambition I wish for. To that I'll climb or fall. My blood's on fire."

Alone, Giovanni talked to himself in a room in Florio's house.

Giovanni said, "Busy opinion is an idle fool that, just like a school rod keeps a child in awe, frightens the inexperienced temper of the mind."

In other words, the common opinion concerning morality influences people's behavior, but experience can show that the popular opinion is wrong.

He continued, "So did it me. Before my precious sister was married, I thought that all taste of love would die in such a contract, but I find no change of pleasure in this formal law of sports."

Giovanni had thought that once his sister was married, he would cease to have any sexual interest in her, but his actual experience was that he was still sexually interested in his sister despite her marriage. In other words, not only was he willing to commit incest with his sister, but also he was willing to commit adultery with her.

He continued, "She is still one and the same to me, and every kiss is as sweet and as delicious as the first I reaped, when the privilege of youth still gave her the title of 'virgin.'

"Oh, the glory of two united hearts like hers and mine! Let men who pore over books dream of other worlds. My world, and all of my happiness, is here, and I'd not change it for the best and eternal life to come. A life of pleasure is Elysium."

Elysium is the pagan Heaven.

Friar Bonaventura entered the room.

Seeing him, Giovanni said, "Father, you enter on the jubilee — the height — of my secluded and private delights. Now I can tell you that the Hell you have often prompted me to think about is nothing other than slavish and foolish superstitious fears and I could prove it, too."

"Thy blindness slays thee," Friar Bonaventura said. "Look at this letter. It is written to thee."

Friar Bonaventura gave Giovanni the letter.

"From whom is it?" Giovanni asked.

"Unrip the seals and see," Friar Bonaventura said.

As Giovanni read Annabella's letter, Friar Bonaventura thought about him, *The blood's yet seething hot that will soon be frozen harder than congealed coral.*

People in this society thought that coral was a sea plant that hardened when it was exposed to the air.

Friar Bonaventura asked, "Why do you change color, son?"

"Before Heaven," Giovanni said, "you make some petty-devil intermediary between my love — Annabella — and your religion-masked sorceries. Where did you get this?"

He did not want to believe that his sister had voluntarily written the letter; instead, he preferred to believe that Friar Bonaventura was an agent of the devil.

Friar Bonaventura said, "Your conscience, youth, is seared and unable to feel, or else thou would stoop to warning. If your conscience were doing what it is supposed to do, you would reform."

"This is her handwriting, I know it, and it is all written in her blood," Giovanni said. "She writes I know not what. Death! I'll not fear an armed thunderbolt aimed at my heart. She writes that our incest has been discovered — a pox on dreams of low faint-hearted cowardice! Discovered? The devil we are! How is it possible? Have Annabella and I grown traitors to our own delights?"

Of course, two other people had known about their incest: Putana and Friar Bonaventura.

Giovanni continued, "May damnation take such dotage, such nonsense, such senile ramblings! This letter is only forged. This is your peevish chattering, weak old man!"

He believed, or wanted to believe, that Friar Bonaventura had forged the letter and Annabella's handwriting.

Vasques entered the room.

Giovanni asked him, "Now, sir, what news do you bring?"

Vasques said, "My lord, according to his yearly custom, is keeping this day a feast in honor of his birthday, and by me he invites you to attend. Your worthy father, along with the Pope's reverend Nuncio, aka the Pope's ambassador, and other nobles of Parma have promised their presence. Will it please you to be one of the number?"

"Yes," Giovanni said, "tell him I dare to come."

"Dare to come?" Vasques asked.

"So I said," Giovanni replied, "and tell him in addition I will come."

"These words are strange to me," Vasques said.

"Say that I will come," Giovanni said.

"You will not fail to come?" Vasques asked.

"Yet more questions!" Giovanni complained. "I'll come, sir. Do you have your answer now?"

Vasques said, "So I'll render my service to you. I will give him your message."

He exited.

"You will not go, I trust," Friar Bonaventura said.

"Not go!" Giovanni said. "Why not?"

"Oh, do not go," Friar Bonaventura urged. "This feast, I'll wager my life, is only a plot to entice you to your ruin. Take my advice and don't go."

"Not go!" Giovanni said. "Even if Death stood and threatened me with his armies of confounding plagues and with hosts of dangers as hot as blazing stars, I would be there."

"Blazing stars" are comets, which were considered omens of danger.

He continued, "Not go! Yes, I will go and I resolve to strike as deep in slaughter as they all will, for I will go."

"Go where thou will," Friar Bonaventura said. "I see the wildness of thy fate draws to an end — to a bad and fearful end.

"I must not stay here and wait to know thy fall. Back to Bologna I with all speed will hasten, and I will shun this coming blow. Parma, farewell. I wish I had never known thee, or anything of thine!

"Well, young man, since no prayer can make thee safe, I leave thee to despair."

Friar Bonaventura exited.

Alone, Giovanni said to himself, "Despair, or tortures of a thousand Hells — all's one to me. I have set up my rest. I have made my final resolution. I will bet all I have."

By "set up his rest," he also meant that he was willing to die.

He continued, "Now, now, work serious thoughts on baneful plots. Be all a man, my soul. Let not the curse of old moral prescriptions rend from me the gall of courage, which enrolls and honorably records a glorious death. If I must totter like a well-grown oak, some shrubs shall in my weighty fall be crushed to splinters; with me they all shall perish!"

The moral prescriptions were those against murdering hosts, against adultery, and against incest.

Deuteronomy 27:22 states, "*Cursed be he that lieth with his sister, the daughter of his father, or the daughter of his mother. And all the people shall say, Amen*" (King James Version).

Leviticus 20:17 states, "*And if a man shall take his sister, his father's daughter, or his mother's daughter, and see her nakedness, and she see his nakedness; it is a wicked thing; and they shall be cut off in the sight of their people: he hath uncovered his sister's nakedness; he shall bear his iniquity*" (King James Version).

Soranzo and Vasques, holding masks, conferred with each other and some bandits in a hall in Soranzo's home.

Soranzo asked the bandits, "You will not fail or shrink in the attempt?"

"I will vouch that they will do their parts," Vasques said to Soranzo.

Vasques then said to the bandits, "Be sure, my masters, to be bloody enough, and as unmerciful as if you were preying upon a rich group of travelers going through the mountains of Liguria. As for your pardons, trust to my lord, but as for reward, you shall trust none but your own pockets."

The bandits said, "We'll commit murder."

Soranzo said, "Here's gold."

He gave them money and then said, "Here's more money; lack for nothing. What you will do is noble and an act of brave revenge. I'll make you rich, bandits, and I'll make you all free."

The bandits shouted, "Liberty! Liberty!"

A pardon would allow them to safely return to places ruled by law.

Vasques said, "Wait, every man take a mask."

Soranzo and Vasques handed out the masks.

Vasques then said to the bandits, "When you are withdrawn, stay as silent as you possibly can. You know the watchword, aka cue. Until it is spoken, don't move, but when you hear that, rush in like a stormy flood. I need not instruct you in your own profession."

The bandits agreed, "No. No. No."

Vasques said, "Go in, then; your purposes are profit and preferment. Leave now!"

The bandits exited.

Soranzo asked, "The guests will all come, Vasques?"

"Yes, sir," Vasques said. "And now let me a little strengthen and sharpen your resolution. You see that nothing is unready for the accomplishment of this great work, except a great — pregnant with revenge — mind in you. Call to your remembrance your disgraces, your loss of honor, and Hippolita's blood thirst for revenge, and arm your courage in your own wrongs. That way you shall best right those wrongs with vengeance that you may truly call your own."

"It is well," Soranzo said. "The less I speak, the more I burn, and blood shall quench that flame of anger."

Vasques said, "Now you begin to turn Italian."

The Italians had a reputation for taking vengeance.

Vasques continued, "This also we must talk about. When my young incest-monger — Giovanni — comes, he will be sharp set on his old bit: He will want to sleep with his sister. Give him time enough to do so, and let him have the liberty of using your chamber and bed. Let my hot and horny hare have a head start before he is hunted to his death, so that, if it should be possible, he goes posthaste to Hell in the very act of his damnation."

Vasques wanted to damn Giovanni's soul as well as kill his body. If Giovanni were killed in or soon after the act of sinning, he would not be able to repent his sin, and his soul would go to Hell.

"It shall be so," Soranzo said. "We will do what you say."

He saw Giovanni walking toward them and said to Vasques, "Look. Just as we would wish, he himself arrives first."

He then said to Giovanni, "Welcome, my much-loved brother-in-law. Now I perceive that you honor me; you are welcome. But where's my father-in-law? Where's Florio?"

Giovanni replied, "With the other statesmen, waiting for the Nuncio of the Pope, to attend upon him here."

He then asked, "How's my sister?"

"Like a good housewife, scarcely ready yet," Soranzo said. "It is best for you to walk to her chamber."

Giovanni said, "If you will."

Soranzo said, "I must wait for my honorable friends. Good brother, get your sister and bring her here."

Giovanni said, "I will. I see that you are busy, sir."

Giovanni exited.

Vasques said, "This is even as the great devil himself would have it! Let him go and glut himself in his own destruction."

Trumpets sounded to announce the arrival of an important guest.

Vasques said to Soranzo, "Listen, the Cardinal has arrived; good sir, be ready to receive him."

The Cardinal, Florio, Donado, the disguised Richardetto, and some attendants arrived.

Soranzo said to the Cardinal, "Most reverend lord, this grace — the honor you do me by attending my feast — has made me proud that you deign to visit my house. I will forever remain your humble servant because of this noble favor."

"You are our friend, my lord," the Cardinal said. "His Holiness the Pope shall understand how zealously you honor Saint Peter's vicar in his substitute. We give our special love to you."

Saint Peter's vicar is the Pope; the Pope's substitute is his Nuncio, aka ambassador — the Cardinal himself.

Soranzo said, "Signiors, to you I give my welcome, and my ever best of thanks for this so memorable courtesy."

He then asked the Cardinal, "Will it please your grace to walk inside?"

The Cardinal replied, "My lord, we come to celebrate your feast with civil, well-behaved merrymaking, as ancient custom teaches. We will go inside."

"Attend his grace there," Soranzo said.

He added, "Signiors, walk this way."

He led them inside.

Annabella, who was richly dressed in the clothing she had worn at her wedding, and Giovanni spoke together in her bedchamber.

"What! Have you changed your mind so soon!" Giovanni complained. "Has your new sprightly lord found out a trick in night-games more than we could know in our simplicity? Does he especially satisfy you in bed? Is he a better lover than I am? Ha! Is that what has happened? Or does the fit come on you to prove treacherous to your past vows and oaths of loyalty to me?"

Annabella asked, "Why should you jest at my distressful calamity, without any sense of the approaching dangers you are in?"

Giovanni said, "What danger's half as great as thy revolt against and disloyalty to me? Thou are a faithless sister, or else thou would know that malice, or any other treachery, would stoop to my bent brows. They would submit when they saw me frown. Why, I hold fate clasped in my fist, and I could command the course of time's eternal motion, if thou had been just a little steadier than an ebbing sea. And what now? Have you now resolved to be chaste and honest?"

"Brother, dear brother," Annabella said, "know what I have been, and know that now there's but a dining-time between us and our destruction, so let's not waste these precious hours in vain and useless speech."

Annabella believed that she and her brother would be murdered during or just after the banquet.

"Alas!" she said. "This gay clothing I and others have put on was not put on except for some special purpose. This sudden ceremonious feast was not put on to waste money. I who have been chambered here alone, barred from my guardian and everyone else, am not for nothing at an instant freed and given fresh access to see other people. Don't be deceived, my brother. This banquet is a harbinger of death to you and me; assure yourself that it is a harbinger of death, and be prepared to welcome death."

Giovanni said, "Well, then. The schoolmen teach that all this globe of earth shall be consumed to ashes in a minute."

Annabella said, "I have read that, too."

Giovanni said, "But except that it is somewhat strange to see the waters burn, I could believe this might be true."

Revelation 21:1 states, "*And I saw a new heaven and a new earth: for the first heaven and the first earth were passed away; and there was no more sea*" (King James Version).

In Book 20, Chapter 16, of his *City of God*, Saint Augustine wondered what would happen to the sea when the first earth passed away. Would it be evaporated by fire that destroyed the first earth, or would it be transformed into something else?

Here is the passage as translated by Marcus Dods:

As for the statement, And there shall be no more sea, I would not lightly say whether it is dried up with that excessive heat, or is itself also turned into some better thing.

Some scholars felt that the earth and sea would be consumed in an instant. In such a case, Giovanni would say that the sea itself burned.

Giovanni continued, "I could believe as well there might be Hell or Heaven."

Annabella said, "It's completely certain that Hell and Heaven exist."

Giovanni said, "A dream! A dream! Otherwise, in this other world we would know one another."

"So we shall," Annabella said.

"Have you heard so?" Giovanni asked.

"Yes," Annabella said. "For certain."

"But do you think," Giovanni asked, "that I shall see you there?

"You look with surprise at me.

"May we kiss one another, talk idly or laugh, or do as we do here?"

The word "do" meant 1) behave, and/or 2) have sex.

Annabella said, "I don't know that. But, good brother, concerning the present time, how do you intend to free yourself from danger? Think of some way by which you can escape; I'm sure the guests have come."

Giovanni said, "Look up, look here; what do you see here in my face?"

Annabella replied, "Mental disturbance and a troubled conscience."

Giovanni said, "Death, and a swift discontented wrath. Continue to look: What do you see in my eyes?"

Annabella replied, "I think you are crying."

"I do cry, indeed," Giovanni said. "These are the funeral tears shed on your grave. These tears furrowed my cheeks when I loved for the first time and did not know how to woo. Beautiful Annabella, if I should here repeat the story of my life, we might lose time."

He then said, "All the spirits of the air, and all things else that are, be the recorders that the tribute which my heart has paid — day and night, early and late — to Annabella's sacred love has been these tears, which are her mourners now!"

These spirits of the air are not Christian.

He continued, "Never until now has Nature done her best to show a matchless beauty to the world — a beauty that in an instant, before it scarcely was seen, the jealous Fates required again."

According to Giovanni, the Fates require that Annabella die so that her beauty can return to whence it came.

"Pray, Annabella, pray!" Giovanni said. "Since we must part, go thou, white in thy soul, to fill a throne of innocence and sanctity in Heaven. Pray, pray, my sister!"

Giovanni was referring to a Neoplatonic view that the sins of the body could not sully the soul; however, this was not the orthodox Christian view.

Because Annabella had sincerely repented her sin, however, she was in fact white in her soul — sinners who sincerely repent receive God's mercy. This is the orthodox Christian view.

Annabella said, "Now I see your drift."

She believed that Giovanni now realized that the banquet would soon be the scene where he and she would be murdered, and she believed that he was asking her to pray to cleanse her soul for Heaven.

She prayed, "You blessed angels, guard me!"

"I say the same thing," Giovanni said. "Kiss me."

They kissed.

He continued, "If ever the aftertimes should hear of our fast-knit affections, though perhaps the laws of conscience and of civil use — civilized behavior — may justly blame us, yet when they only know our love for each other, that love will remove the shame of that sexual passion that would be abhorred in other cases of incest.

"Give me your hand."

Looking at it, he said, "How sweetly life runs in these well-colored veins! How confidently these palms promise health! But I could criticize Nature because of this cunning flattery."

Her hand's appearance promised health, but Giovanni knew that the promise would soon be broken.

"Kiss me again," he said. "Forgive me."

"With my heart," Annabella said.

"Farewell!" Giovanni said.

"Will you be gone?" Annabella asked. "Are you leaving?"

"Be dark, bright sun," Giovanni said, "and turn this mid-day to night so that thy gilt rays may not behold a deed that will make their splendor more sooty than the poets write that their Styx is!"

The Styx is a river in Hades, Land of the Dead.

"One more kiss, my sister," Giovanni said.

"What do you mean by this?" Annabella asked.

Giovanni replied, "I intend to save thy reputation, and kill thee in a kiss."

As he kissed her, he stabbed her and said, "Thus die, and die by me, and by my hand! Revenge is mine; honor commands love."

Giovanni had said, "Revenge is mine"; however, scripture says differently.

Romans 12:19 states, "*Dearly beloved, avenge not yourselves, but rather give place unto wrath: for it is written, Vengeance is mine; I will repay, saith the Lord*" (King James Version).

The words "*give place unto wrath*" mean "let God's righteous wrath take care of things."

Annabella said, "Oh, brother, I die by your hand!"

Giovanni said, "When thou are dead, I'll give my reasons for causing your death, for to dispute with thy — even in thy death — most lovely beauty, would make me stagger and hesitate to perform this act that I most glory in."

Annabella prayed, "Forgive him, Heaven —"

In Luke 23:34, some of Jesus' last words asked God to forgive those who killed Him:

"*Then said Jesus, Father, forgive them; for they know not what they do*" (King James Version).

She added, "— and forgive me my sins!"

God forgives sincerely repented sins even when the sinner repents in the final moment of the sinner's life.

She then said, "Farewell, my brother. You are unkind, unkind — you don't act like a brother should act."'

She spoke the truth.

She prayed, "Have mercy, great Heaven!"

Then she moaned and died.

Giovanni said to himself, "She's dead, alas, good soul! The hapless fruit that in her womb received its life from me has had from me a cradle and a grave."

He had killed both his sister and their unborn baby.

He continued, "I must not dally — this sad marriage-bed in all her best bore her both alive and dead."

According to Giovanni, she was best as a lover in bed. In addition, she was now wearing her best clothing — the clothing she was married in.

He then said, "Soranzo, thou have missed thy target in this! I have forestalled now thy far-reaching plots, and killed a love whom for each drop of her blood I would have pawned my heart.

"Beautiful Annabella, how beautiful beyond measure are thou in thy wounds, triumphing over infamy and hate!

"Shrink not, courageous hand; stand up, my heart, and boldly act my last, and greater part!"

The Cardinal, Florio, Donado, Soranzo, the disguised Richardetto, Vasques, and some attendants stood in a banqueting room in Soranzo's house.

Vasques and Soranzo were apart from the others, and so they could talk privately and quietly together.

Vasques said, "Remember, sir, what you have to do; be wise and resolute."

"Say no more," Soranzo said. "My heart is fixed."

He then said loudly to the Cardinal, "Will it please your grace to taste these simple foods? Although the use of such set entertainments arises more from custom than from cause, yet, reverend sir, I am still in your debt because you honor me with your presence."

He meant that such entertainments were held more as a result of upholding a custom than for any substantial reason.

Using the majestic plural, which high-ranking religious people such as the Pope used, the Cardinal said, "And we are your friend."

Soranzo asked, "But where's Giovanni, my brother-in-law?"

Giovanni, who was bloody, entered the room, holding a dagger on which a human heart was impaled.

"Here I am, here, Soranzo!" Giovanni said. "I am decorated in steaming blood, blood that triumphs over death! I am proud in the spoil of love and vengeance!"

"Spoil" means both 1) destruction, and 2) plunder.

He continued, "Fate, or all the powers that guide the motions of immortal souls, could not prevent me."

"What is the meaning of this?" the Cardinal asked.

"Giovanni!" Florio cried. "My son!"

Soranzo asked himself quietly, "Shall I and my revenge be forestalled?"

"Be not amazed," Giovanni said. "If your apprehensive hearts shrink at a mere sight, what bloodless fear of cowardly emotion would have seized your senses, had you beheld the snatching away of life and beauty that I have done?"

He paused and then said, "My sister! Oh, my sister!"

Florio asked, "What about her?"

"The glory of my deed darkened the midday sun and made noon appear to be night," Giovanni said.

He used the word "glory," but readers might use the word "evil."

He continued, "You came to feast, my lords, with dainty fare, I came to feast, too; but I dug for food in a much richer mine than gold or precious stone of any calculated value. I dug for a heart: a heart, my lords, in which my heart is entombed. Look closely at the heart. Do you recognize it?"

Vasques asked himself quietly, "What strange riddle is this?"

"It is Annabella's heart, it is," Giovanni said. "Why do you startle? I vow that it is her heart — this dagger's point plowed up her fruitful womb, and left to me the fame of a most glorious executioner."

If his words can be taken literally, he had cut into his sister's womb, and he may have seen their dead unborn fetus. Or he may have simply meant that he had stabbed his sister in the abdomen, in which case he may have stabbed their unborn baby.

Florio asked, "Madman, are you in your right mind?"

"Yes, father," Giovanni said, "and, so that times to come may know, listen to how, as my fate, I honored my revenge. Listen, father. To your ears I will tell how much I have deserved to be your son."

By "son," he meant both 1) son and 2) son-in-law.

Florio asked, "What is it that thou are saying?"

Giovanni said, "Nine moons have had their changes, since I first thoroughly viewed, and truly loved, your daughter and my sister."

"What!" Florio said. "Alas, my lords, he is a frantic madman!"

"Father, no, I am not," Giovanni said. "For nine months, in secret, I enjoyed sweet Annabella's sheets; for nine months I lived a happy monarch of her heart and her.

"Soranzo, thou know this; thy paler cheek bears the shaming print of thy disgrace, for her too fruitful womb too soon revealed the happy passage of our stolen delights, and made her mother to a child unborn."

The Cardinal said, "Incestuous villain!"

Florio said, "Oh, his rage — his madness — makes him lie."

"It does not make me lie," Giovanni said. "It is the oracle of truth; I vow that it is so."

"I shall burst with fury!" Soranzo said. "Bring the strumpet forth!"

Vasques said, "I shall, sir."

He exited to get Annabella, if she were still alive.

"Do, sir," Giovanni said. "Have you all no faith to credit yet my triumphs? Here I swear by all that you call sacred, by the love I bore my Annabella while she lived, that these hands have from her bosom ripped this heart."

Vasques returned.

Giovanni asked him, "Is it true or not, sir, that I have ripped my sister's heart from her bosom?"

Vasques said, "It is most strangely true."

Florio said, "Cursed man — have I lived to —"

The shock was too much for him, and he fell and died.

The Cardinal said, "Be strong, Florio."

Realizing that Florio was dead, the Cardinal then said to Giovanni, "Monster of children! See what thou have done! Thou have broken thy old father's heart!"

The Cardinal then asked the others present, "Do any of you dare to restrain him?"

"Let them try!" Giovanni said. "Oh, my father — how well his death becomes him in his griefs! Why, this was done with courage; now survives none of our house but I, gilt in the blood of a fair sister and a hapless father."

"Gilt" means both 1) gilded, and 2) guilt. Giovanni meant only the first meaning. Readers may think the word "guilty" is also applicable.

Soranzo said, "Inhuman scorn of men, do thou think that thou will outlive thy murders?"

He drew his sword.

Giovanni said, "Yes, I tell thee yes. For in my fists I bear the twisted threads of life."

He was identifying himself with the three Fates who spin, measure, and cut the thread of life.

Giovanni then said, "Soranzo, see this heart, which was thy wife's. Thus I exchange it royally for thine heart."

They fought.

Thrusting with his sword, Giovanni said, "And thus and thus! Now brave revenge is mine."

Mortally wounded, Soranzo fell.

"I cannot hold back any longer," Vasques said to Giovanni. "You, sir, are you grown insolent in your butcheries? Let's fight."

"Come," Giovanni said. "I am armed to meet thee."

They fought.

As they fought, Vasques said, "No! Will your death not be yet? If this sword will not kill you, another sword shall. Aren't you dead yet? I shall fix you right now!"

He called, "Vengeance!"

Hearing the prearranged cue for them to render assistance, the bandits rushed in.

"Welcome!" Giovanni said. "Let there come in more of you. Whoever you are, I dare to face your worst."

Vasques and the bandits surrounded and mortally wounded him.

"Oh, I can stand no longer," Giovanni said. "Feeble arms, have you so soon lost your strength?"

He fell.

Vasques said to Giovanni, "Now, you are welcome, sir!"

He then said to the bandits, "Leave, my masters. All is done; shift for yourselves; your reward is your own. Shift for yourselves."

Soranzo was dying; he could not give the bandits pardons.

"Away!" the bandits said. "Away!"

They exited.

Vasques asked the morally wounded Soranzo, "How are you, my lord?"

Vasques pointed to the mortally wounded Giovanni and asked, "Do you see this?"

He then asked again, "How are you?"

"I am dead," Soranzo said, "but in death I am well pleased because I have lived to see my wrongs revenged on that black devil — Giovanni! Oh, Vasques, to thy bosom let me give my last words of breath — don't let that lecher live!"

He moaned and died.

Vasques said, "May the reward of peace and rest be with you, my always dearest lord and master!"

Giovanni asked, "Whose hand gave me this mortal wound?"

Vasques said, "My hand did, sir. I was the first man to wound you. Have you had enough to kill you?"

Giovanni said, "I thank thee. Thou have done to me only what I would have else have done to myself."

According to Catholicism, suicide is a sin.

Giovanni continued, "Are you sure that thy lord is dead?"

"Oh, impudent slave!" Vasques said. "As sure as I am sure to see thee die."

The Cardinal said to Giovanni, "Think on thy life and thy end, and call for mercy."

This was good advice.

"Mercy?" Giovanni said. "Why, I have found it in this justice."

He believed that everything he had done, including committing incest with his sister, and murdering his sister and their unborn child, was just. Because he did not believe that he had sinned, he did not ask God to forgive his sins.

The Cardinal said, "Strive yet to cry to Heaven for mercy."

"Oh, I bleed fast," Giovanni said. "Death, thou are a guest I have long looked for. I embrace thee and thy wounds. Oh, my last minute comes! Wherever I go, let me enjoy this grace — freely to view my Annabella's face."

He died.

His last words were ominous: "Wherever I go, let me enjoy this grace — freely to view my Annabella's face."

If he ended up in Hell, he wanted his sister to also end up in Hell so he could see her face.

Donado said, "Strange miracle of justice!"

The Cardinal said, "Raise up the guards in the city, or we shall all be murdered!"

He was afraid of Vasques, a Spaniard and a servant who had killed someone of a much higher social class.

"You need not fear that," Vasques said. "You need not. This strange task being ended, I have paid the duty to the son that I had vowed to the father."

Vasques had vowed to give his service to Soranzo's father; that service ended with the death of Soranzo, who had left no heirs.

The Cardinal said, "Speak, wretched villain. Tell me what incarnate fiend has led thee on to this?"

Vasques said, "Loyalty, and pity on the wrongs done to my master, for know, my lord, that I am by birth a Spaniard. Lord Soranzo's father brought me out of my country in my youth. While he lived, I served him faithfully. Since

Soranzo's father's death, I have been the servant of Soranzo, as loyal to him as I was to his father. What I have done was done out of duty, and I repent nothing, except that the loss of my life had not ransomed Soranzo's death. I wish that I had been able to die to save his life."

The Cardinal asked, "Tell me, fellow, do thou know of any other person yet unnamed who had knowledge of this incest?"

"Yes," Vasques said. "There is an old woman who was the guardian of this murdered lady."

He meant Putana.

The Cardinal asked, "And what's become of her?"

Vasques pointed out a window to the one-room coal-house and said, "She is inside this room. Her eyes, after her confession, I caused to be put out, but I ordered her to be kept alive so she could confirm what from Giovanni's own mouth you have heard. Now, my lord, what I have done you may be the judge of; and let your own wisdom be a judge of your own justice."

The Cardinal said, "Peace! Quiet! First this woman, chief in these results, my sentence is that forthwith she be taken out of the city, for example's sake, there to be burnt to ashes."

To whom was he referring? Putana, whose testimony he had not heard? She was the chief, and only, accomplice, but Annabella was the chief female actor in sins that had led to these results. Did the Cardinal mean for Annabella's corpse to be taken out and burned?

Note that the Cardinal was blaming females, just as Eve is blamed for the expulsion from the Garden of Eden.

Whomever the Cardinal meant to be burned, it is possible that the person who would carry out the order would not ask him for clarification because the Cardinal caused fear in other people.

Donado said, "This sentence is most just."

The Cardinal said, "Be it your responsibility, Donado. See that it is done."

"I shall," Donado said.

"What about me?" Vasques asked. "If my punishment is death, it is welcome. I have been honest and loyal to the son, as I was to the father."

The Cardinal said, "Fellow, as for thee, since what thou did was done not for thyself, seeing that you are no Italian, we banish thee forever. You must depart within three days. In this we are being merciful because of the circumstances of your actions; we do not condone what you did."

The Cardinal could have sentenced Vasques to death.

"This sentence is good," Vasques said. "This conquest — the death of Giovanni — is mine, and I rejoice that a Spaniard outdid an Italian in revenge."

He exited.

The Cardinal said, "Take up these slaughtered bodies, and see that they are buried. And all the gold and jewels, or whatsoever, we confiscate by the canons of the church. We seize upon them for the Pope's proper use."

Florio, Giovanni, Soranzo, and Annabella had died without heirs.

Richardetto took off his disguise and said, "I beg your grace's pardon. Thus long I have lived disguised so that I could see the effect of pride and lust at once both brought to shameful conclusions."

"What!" the Cardinal said. "Are you Richardetto, whom we thought to be dead?"

Donado began, "Sir, was it you —"

Richardetto interrupted, "I am your friend."

"We shall have time to talk fully about all of this," the Cardinal said, "but never yet have incest and murder so strangely met.

"Of one so young, so rich in nature's gifts and store, who could not say that it's a pity she's a whore?"

Readers should note that Annabella had repented her sins before she died, while Giovanni had not. Only one of these two sinners shall enter Paradise.

APPENDIX A: BIBLIOGRAPHY

John Ford. *'Tis Pity She's a Whore*. eBook.
Folger Shakespeare Library
https://emed.folger.edu/sites/default/files/folger_encodings/pdf/
EMED-TPSW-reg-3.pdf

'Tis Pity She's a Whore. John Ford. *Renaissance drama : an anthology of plays and entertainments*. Edited by Arthur F. Kinney. Malden, Mass.: Blackwell Publishers, 2005.

'Tis Pity She's a Whore. Edited by N. W. Bawcutt. Ford, John, 1586-ca. 1640. Lincoln, Nebraska: University of Nebraska Press, 1966.

'Tis Pity She's a Whore. John Ford. Edited by Simon Barker. London; New York: Routledge, 1997.

'Tis Pity She's a Whore. John Ford. Edited by Derek Roper. Manchester; New York: Manchester University Press ; New York : Distributed in the USA by St. Martin's Press, 1997.

'Tis Pity She's a Whore. John Ford. Edited and introduced by Lisa Hopkins. London: Nick Hern, 2003.

'Tis Pity She's a Whore. John Ford. Edited by Sonia Massai. London: Arden Shakespeare, 2011.

'Tis Pity She's a Whore. *'Tis Pity She's a Whore and Other Plays*. John Ford. Edited by Marion Lomax. Oxford; New York : Oxford University Press, 1995.

***

Source of Saint Augustine Quotation:
Translated by Marcus Dods. From *Nicene and Post-Nicene Fathers, First Series, Vol. 2*. Edited by Philip Schaff. (Buffalo, NY: Christian Literature Publishing Co., 1887.) Revised and edited for New Advent by Kevin Knight.
http://www.newadvent.org/fathers/120120.htm

APPENDIX B: ABOUT THE AUTHOR

It was a dark and stormy night. Suddenly a cry rang out, and on a hot summer night in 1954, Josephine, wife of Carl Bruce, gave birth to a boy — me. Unfortunately, this young married couple allowed Reuben Saturday, Josephine's brother, to name their first-born. Reuben, aka "The Joker," decided that Bruce was a nice name, so he decided to name me Bruce Bruce. I have gone by my middle name — David — ever since.

Being named Bruce David Bruce hasn't been all bad. Bank tellers remember me very quickly, so I don't often have to show an ID. It can be fun in charades, also. When I was a counselor as a teenager at Camp Echoing Hills in Warsaw, Ohio, a fellow counselor gave the signs for "sounds like" and "two words," then she pointed to a bruise on her leg twice. Bruise Bruise? Oh yeah, Bruce Bruce is the answer!

Uncle Reuben, by the way, gave me a haircut when I was in kindergarten. He cut my hair short and shaved a small bald spot on the back of my head. My mother wouldn't let me go to school until the bald spot grew out again.

Of all my brothers and sisters (six in all), I am the only transplant to Athens, Ohio. I was born in Newark, Ohio, and have lived all around Southeastern Ohio. However, I moved to Athens to go to Ohio University and have never left.

At Ohio U, I never could make up my mind whether to major in English or Philosophy, so I got a bachelor's degree with a double major in both areas, then I added a Master of Arts degree in English and a Master of Arts degree in Philosophy. Yes, I have my MAMA degree.

Currently, and for a long time to come (I eat fruits and veggies), I am spending my retirement writing books such as *Nadia Comaneci: Perfect 10*, *The Funniest People in Dance*, *Homer's* Iliad: *A Retelling in Prose*, and *William Shakespeare's* Othello: *A Retelling in Prose*.

By the way, my sister Brenda Kennedy writes romances such as *A New Beginning* and *Shattered Dreams*.

APPENDIX C: SOME BOOKS BY DAVID BRUCE

Retellings of a Classic Work of Literature

Arden of Faversham: *A Retelling*

Ben Jonson's The Alchemist: *A Retelling*

Ben Jonson's The Arraignment, or Poetaster: *A Retelling*

Ben Jonson's Bartholomew Fair: *A Retelling*

Ben Jonson's The Case is Altered: *A Retelling*

Ben Jonson's Catiline's Conspiracy: *A Retelling*

Ben Jonson's The Devil is an Ass: *A Retelling*

Ben Jonson's Epicene: *A Retelling*

Ben Jonson's Every Man in His Humor: *A Retelling*

Ben Jonson's Every Man Out of His Humor: *A Retelling*

Ben Jonson's The Fountain of Self-Love, or Cynthia's Revels: *A Retelling*

Ben Jonson's The Magnetic Lady, or Humors Reconciled: *A Retelling*

Ben Jonson's The New Inn, or The Light Heart: *A Retelling*

Ben Jonson's Sejanus' Fall: *A Retelling*

Ben Jonson's The Staple of News: *A Retelling*

Ben Jonson's A Tale of a Tub: *A Retelling*

Ben Jonson's Volpone, or the Fox: *A Retelling*

Christopher Marlowe's Complete Plays: Retellings

Christopher Marlowe's Dido, Queen of Carthage: *A Retelling*

Christopher Marlowe's Doctor Faustus: *Retellings of the 1604 A-Text and of the 1616 B-Text*

Christopher Marlowe's Edward II: *A Retelling*

Christopher Marlowe's The Massacre at Paris: *A Retelling*

Christopher Marlowe's The Rich Jew of Malta: *A Retelling*

Christopher Marlowe's Tamburlaine, Parts 1 and 2: *Retellings*

Dante's Divine Comedy: *A Retelling in Prose*

Dante's Inferno: *A Retelling in Prose*

Dante's Purgatory: *A Retelling in Prose*

Dante's Paradise: *A Retelling in Prose*

The Famous Victories of Henry V: *A Retelling*

From the Iliad *to the* Odyssey: *A Retelling in Prose of Quintus of Smyrna's* Posthomerica

George Chapman, Ben Jonson, and John Marston's Eastward Ho! *A Retelling*

George Peele's The Arraignment of Paris: *A Retelling*

George Peele's The Battle of Alcazar: *A Retelling*

George's Peele's David and Bathsheba, and the Tragedy of Absalom: *A Retelling*

George Peele's Edward I: *A Retelling*

George Peele's The Old Wives' Tale: *A Retelling*

George-a-Greene: *A Retelling*

The History of King Leir: *A Retelling*

Homer's Iliad: *A Retelling in Prose*

Homer's Odyssey: *A Retelling in Prose*

J.W. Gent.'s The Valiant Scot: *A Retelling*

Jason and the Argonauts: A Retelling in Prose of Apollonius of Rhodes' Argonautica

John Ford: Eight Plays Translated into Modern English

John Ford's The Broken Heart: *A Retelling*

John Ford's The Fancies, Chaste and Noble: *A Retelling*

John Ford's The Lady's Trial: *A Retelling*

John Ford's The Lover's Melancholy: *A Retelling*

John Ford's Love's Sacrifice: *A Retelling*

John Ford's Perkin Warbeck: *A Retelling*

John Ford's The Queen: *A Retelling*

John Ford's 'Tis Pity She's a Whore: *A Retelling*

John Lyly's Campaspe: *A Retelling*

John Lyly's Endymion, The Man in the Moon: *A Retelling*

John Lyly's Galatea: *A Retelling*

John Lyly's Love's Metamorphosis: *A Retelling*

John Lyly's Midas: *A Retelling*

John Lyly's Mother Bombie: *A Retelling*

John Lyly's Sappho and Phao: *A Retelling*

John Lyly's The Woman in the Moon: *A Retelling*

John Webster's The White Devil: *A Retelling*

King Edward III: *A Retelling*

Mankind: *A Medieval Morality Play* (A Retelling)

Margaret Cavendish's The Unnatural Tragedy: *A Retelling*

The Merry Devil of Edmonton: *A Retelling*

The Summoning of Everyman: *A Medieval Morality Play* (A Retelling)

Robert Greene's Friar Bacon and Friar Bungay: *A Retelling*

The Taming of a Shrew: *A Retelling*

Tarlton's Jests: A Retelling

Thomas Middleton's A Chaste Maid in Cheapside: *A Retelling*

Thomas Middleton's Women Beware Women: *A Retelling*

Thomas Middleton and Thomas Dekker's The Roaring Girl: *A Retelling*

Thomas Middleton and William Rowley's The Changeling: *A Retelling*

The Trojan War and Its Aftermath: Four Ancient Epic Poems

Virgil's Aeneid: *A Retelling in Prose*

William Shakespeare's 5 Late Romances: Retellings in Prose

William Shakespeare's 10 Histories: Retellings in Prose

William Shakespeare's 11 Tragedies: Retellings in Prose

William Shakespeare's 12 Comedies: Retellings in Prose

William Shakespeare's 38 Plays: Retellings in Prose
William Shakespeare's 1 Henry IV, aka Henry IV, Part 1: *A Retelling in Prose*
William Shakespeare's 2 Henry IV, aka Henry IV, Part 2: *A Retelling in Prose*
William Shakespeare's 1 Henry VI, aka Henry VI, Part 1: *A Retelling in Prose*
William Shakespeare's 2 Henry VI, aka Henry VI, Part 2: *A Retelling in Prose*
William Shakespeare's 3 Henry VI, aka Henry VI, Part 3: *A Retelling in Prose*
William Shakespeare's All's Well that Ends Well: *A Retelling in Prose*
William Shakespeare's Antony and Cleopatra: *A Retelling in Prose*
William Shakespeare's As You Like It: *A Retelling in Prose*
William Shakespeare's The Comedy of Errors: *A Retelling in Prose*
William Shakespeare's Coriolanus: *A Retelling in Prose*
William Shakespeare's Cymbeline: *A Retelling in Prose*
William Shakespeare's Hamlet: *A Retelling in Prose*
William Shakespeare's Henry V: *A Retelling in Prose*
William Shakespeare's Henry VIII: *A Retelling in Prose*
William Shakespeare's Julius Caesar: *A Retelling in Prose*
William Shakespeare's King John: *A Retelling in Prose*
William Shakespeare's King Lear: *A Retelling in Prose*
William Shakespeare's Love's Labor's Lost: *A Retelling in Prose*
William Shakespeare's Macbeth: *A Retelling in Prose*
William Shakespeare's Measure for Measure: *A Retelling in Prose*
William Shakespeare's The Merchant of Venice: *A Retelling in Prose*
William Shakespeare's The Merry Wives of Windsor: *A Retelling in Prose*
William Shakespeare's A Midsummer Night's Dream: *A Retelling in Prose*
William Shakespeare's Much Ado About Nothing: *A Retelling in Prose*
William Shakespeare's Othello: *A Retelling in Prose*
William Shakespeare's Pericles, Prince of Tyre: *A Retelling in Prose*
William Shakespeare's Richard II: *A Retelling in Prose*
William Shakespeare's Richard III: *A Retelling in Prose*
William Shakespeare's Romeo and Juliet: *A Retelling in Prose*
William Shakespeare's The Taming of the Shrew: *A Retelling in Prose*
William Shakespeare's The Tempest: *A Retelling in Prose*
William Shakespeare's Timon of Athens: *A Retelling in Prose*
William Shakespeare's Titus Andronicus: *A Retelling in Prose*
William Shakespeare's Troilus and Cressida: *A Retelling in Prose*
William Shakespeare's Twelfth Night: *A Retelling in Prose*
William Shakespeare's The Two Gentlemen of Verona: *A Retelling in Prose*
William Shakespeare's The Two Noble Kinsmen: *A Retelling in Prose*
William Shakespeare's The Winter's Tale: *A Retelling in Prose*